Penny's
Cove

Penny's Cove

A New England Novel

Sharon Snow Sirois

LIGHTHOUSE PUBLISHING

North Haven, Connecticut

LIGHTHOUSE PUBLISHING
P.O. Box 396
North Haven, CT 06473

This book is a work of fiction. The names, characters,
dialogue, and plot are either the products of the author's
imagination or used fictitiously. Any resemblance
to places, events, or persons, living or dead, is entirely
coincidental and unintentional by the author or publisher.

Illustration by Beverly Rich
Computer Graphics by Jane Lyman

All Scripture quotations are from the Holy Bible,
New International Version ©1978 by
N.Y. International Bible Society, used by permission of
Zondervan Publishing House

Library of Congress Control Number 2003091354

International Standard Book Number 0-9679052-4-9

Printed in the United States of America

*I am so incredibly thankful to be able to serve God
through my writing. I want to be a spotlight shining on Him
so others may see Him and be lifted up and see
how truly awesome the God is that we serve.
May He receive all the glory and praise in my life.
He is the one who has given me true life
and He is the one that I live for.*

*"But as for me, it is good to be near God. I have made
the Sovereign Lord my refuge; I will tell of all your deeds."*
PSALM 73:28

To the Readers

Dear Friends,

I want to thank you so much for all your letters and emails. I have always enjoyed the penpal relationship. I was the typical little kid that came home from camp with stacks of addresses. My first paying job was created for me by one of my elderly cousins so I could earn enough money to buy stamps to keep in touch with all my camp friends that were spread across the country. Hearing from you all is encouraging and basically just a whole lot of fun. Thank you for taking the time to write. I love hearing from you and appreciate the fact that you've taken time out of your day to read my book.

When many of you write, you mention that you are praying for me. I want to thank you for your prayers. I value them greatly. They are a wonderful gift to me and mean more than words can say. Prayer is powerful. God honors our prayers and carries us through life in a way that nothing else can.

Penny's Cove is the fifth book in the New England Novel Series. The next half a dozen books will be a continuing story, based on a place that I absolutely love. Lake Winnipesaukee, which is New England's largest lake, is twenty-six miles long and fifteen miles wide. It's located in the Lake Region of New Hampshire, right at the foothills of the beautiful White Mountains.

Lake Winnipesaukee has so many individually unique aspects to it, as a writer, it throws my mind into creative overdrive. The lake itself really does have over three hundred islands. That alone is a fun thing to write about, but along with that, Lake Winnipesaukee has the only U. S. Mail Boat in the entire country that is still actively operating. Since 1892, boats have delivered mail on this lake. In 1916, an act of Congress made this the only floating post office on an inland body of water in the United States of America.

Some boats carry mail to pass onto other boats. That's considered a delivery service. To qualify as an actual floating post office, the boat has to have an official United States Postmaster on board and have an actual postal route with specific stops. The U. S. Mail Boat also cancels the mail right aboard the boat.

Back in the 1800's, the mail was delivered on the lake by a horse boat. In the 1960's, the mail was delivered by a retired Naval P.T. boat. The names and styles of the mail boats have changed over the years, but the service they provided hasn't. They deliver the U. S. mail to the many islands, in all kinds of weather, and if the mail happens to fall into the lake, the postmaster swims for it!

The Mail Boat delivers mail, among other items, to the many islands. If you pay a fare, you can ride the Mail Boat route and visit the islands up close and personal. I've done this with my family many times. Each time is an adventure unique and different, and I'd highly recommend this journey to anyone who visits the lake. It has always been a highlight for us not to mention the entertaining, quick-witted, amusing dialogue by the postmaster himself. To hear his thick Boston accent along with his stories about the lake and islands is worth the ride itself.

Lake Winnipesaukee's floating post office has received mail in many different ways. The most common is to pick it up in the mail houses on the different islands. One of the more unusual ways is for boats to approach him on the lake with mail. The postmaster has even taken mail from the extended hand of a water-skier passing by. I would have loved to have seen that!

As you journey through *Penny's Cove*, you will meet many characters along the way. You will share in their triumphs as well as their sorrows. Meghan Kane sees first hand that God is a father to the fatherless. He is the one we should place our trust in. Many promises out in the world can be empty and vain. Disappointment has flooded through all of us at times when we have placed our trust in someone who didn't deserve it. I encourage you to put your trust in God. He is faithful and good and His promises are always true. Never once throughout the Bible did He ever go back on His word. He is faithful to guide and carry you through this life. Turn to Him and trust in Him today.

Thank you again for your prayers and letters. I really am very humbled by them. I hope you enjoy our time together and your visit to New Hampshire's Lake Winnipesaukee.

God Bless,
Sharon Snow Sirois

I love to hear from my readers!
You can write me through Lighthouse Publishing, P.O. Box 396, North Haven, CT 06473 or email me at sharonsnowsirois@hotmail.com

"A father to the fatherless,
a defender of the widows,
is God in His holy dwelling."

PSALM 68:5

Acknowledgments

Lighthouse Publishing. I feel so honored to work with such a talented group of people. Your expertise in each area shines brightly and helps make these books the best they can be. Thank you for all your time and dedication.

Editorial Staff. Patricia Stearns and William Burrill. What a wonderful team you are! I have enjoyed every minute of our time together. Thank you so much for all your long hours and dedication to making this book the best it can be. Thank you for your prayers and encouragement along the way. You are both very talented, and it is my privilege to work with you. You are a blessing!

Beverly Rich. Thank you for your beautiful illustration. You really amaze me with your talent. I love the lighthouse and the cottage. I'm packing up my family and we're moving in! The painting is just beautiful!

Jane Lyman. You do an excellent job with the computer graphics. All your time and attention to the little details keep us going. Thank you for your time and patience. You're outstanding at what you do.

The Snow & Sirois Families. You guys are an incredible support system for all of us. You cheer us on, through thick and thin, listen to all the updates along the way and never stop encouraging us. Thank you for all your prayers and encouragement. I love you!

Peter. You are such a wonderful husband, father and best friend. You always go the extra mile, put in the additional time to make our marriage and family the best it can be. Your love, prayers and support carry me through so much. You're one in a million, and I treasure you and love you with all my heart.

Jennifer, John, Robert, Michael. What an incredible blessing it is for me to be your mom. I'd always dreamed about what it would be like to be a mom when I grew up, but you guys far exceeded any dreams I ever had! You're the coolest little group of prayer warriors that I've ever met. You cheer us tough our victories and pray us through the though times. You are special beyond words, and I love you with all my heart!

This one is for my sister,
Elizabeth Snow

A special bond is shared between sisters that runs deep and wide. It's filled with love, friendship, unconditional support and forgiveness. It is a relationship that is virtually unbreakable.

Looking back on my childhood, it suddenly hit me that you were my first real friend. How many people can say that they are still close to their first true friend and that friend is still a very best friend?

We shared so much of our lives together because we were only sixteen months apart. I can't think of a single childhood memory that you weren't a part of. I couldn't imagine a better older sister. You were always there for me; defending, protecting, listening and loving. You stood by me, stood up for me and stepped in when I needed you to.

You always played such a huge part in my life. Often times you understood me when I didn't even understand myself. You believed in me when I didn't have an ounce of courage to believe in myself. You helped me deal with life's pressures and all the up's and down's it brings. You never offered loads of unwanted advice; you gave me something much better. You gave me your love and your prayers. When you said that you'd pray for me, I knew it wasn't some polite gesture. I always knew you were really praying for me.

I always felt safe trusting you with my deepest concerns, highest hopes, and wildest dreams. I never had to worry about weighing my words with you. I could speak honestly from my heart, knowing what I said to you would never travel anywhere. There is so much peace and freedom in that. What a treasure and gift it is to know someone so well that you can just be yourself with them.

The older I become, the more I see how truly unusual our friendship is. It is a friendship that has withstood the test of time, change and distance. No matter how many miles we are apart; my heart will always be close to yours. You are loving, loyal and faithful to the end. You never bail out on anyone. You are a trusted confidant.

You were and still are an incredible support system. You taught me never to back down to a challenge. You always taught me never to look at the world through my eyes and intellect but through the heart that God has given me. That's how you see life clearly. You told me that my job wasn't to make sense of God's ways; it was simply to follow them.

I know in all my journeys still to come, I could never find a truer friend to walk them with. I have always been so proud to call you my friend, but I'm even prouder to call you my sister. I love you with all my heart.

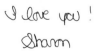

Prologue

As the U.S. Mail boat glided through the crystal clear waters of Lake Winnipesaukee, Daniel turned and studied his father for a moment. Peter Hatch, the Captain of the Sally G., was almost as well-known and well-loved throughout the state of New Hampshire as his beloved mail boat. Being the captain of the last running U.S. Mail boat in the entire country had made Peter Hatch and the Sally G. legendary. It had given his father a celebrity status that few people remaining in a non-celebrity job knew.

Daniel turned his head and gazed out across the lake that was dotted by more than three hundred little islands. As his eyes drifted upwards, he smiled at the way that the White Mountains of New Hampshire surrounded Lake Winnipesaukee as though they were giving the lake a gentle hug. He marveled at how the White Mountains could seem so friendly and breathtakingly awesome at the same time. They were two extremes coming together to form perfect mountains. Peaks and valleys, summits and base camps, mountaintops and lows, the White Mountains had it all.

Daniel turned and saw his father smiling at him, and he smiled right back. He didn't think anyone could feel closer to his father than he did. "You've got a great job, Dad."

Peter Hatch smiled. "The best. Do you think that you might be interested in taking my place someday?"

Daniel grinned. "Dad, I don't want to take your place, I want to become your co-pilot. I like working with you. I think we make a great team."

Peter gazed lovingly at his son. "We do make a good team, Daniel. I love working with you too."

From his dad's tall, stocky frame, all the way down to his broad welcoming grin, Daniel understood fully why people constantly remarked on their likenesses. His own mom often said that he was a little carbon copy of his father in both appearance and personality.

Daniel felt fairly confident that he would have the same gray highlights in his black hair when he reached his mid-forties as his father had. He only hoped they made him look as wise and dignified as his father did. He loved his dad deeply and wanted to grow up to be just like him.

As the mail boat approached the group of islands known as the Christmas Islands, Daniel grabbed the mailbag for Bethlehem Island. He went out and stood on the deck of the boat, waiting for the Sally G. to pull up to the town dock. When the boat was about three feet from the dock, he backed up and made a flying leap that landed him smack in the center of the dock. He turned his head as he heard his father's laughter.

"You know Son, if you don't make the jump, you'll not only get wet but you'll be swimming for the mail."

Daniel laughed. "I haven't had to swim for the mail in months, dad. I think my timing is getting better."

Mr. Hatch laughed again. He found his son's antics amusing. "I know, but just remember that the water is a lot colder than it looks."

Father and son walked to the green and white mailbox house located on the far corner of the town dock. They immediately set out delivering the mail to the appropriate mailboxes. Every resident on the island had a box and over the years, the father and son team had developed a standard pattern for doing the job quickly and efficiently. Mr. Hatch always took the top mailboxes while Daniel stuffed the lower ones. They could deliver the mail to all fifty boxes and be off for their next island stop within twenty minutes.

Back aboard the Sally G., Mr. Hatch steered his boat toward Jerusalem Island. Daniel walked over and stood next to his dad. His hands were shoved deep into his navy blue pants and he stared ahead aimlessly, watching their next stop come into view.

"Is there something that you want to talk to me about, Son?" Mr. Hatch asked gently.

Daniel nodded. "Yes, Dad, " he answered slowly.

Mr. Hatch set his coffee cup down and turned his full attention to his son. The hesitancy in Daniel's voice as well as the struggle of emotion parading across his face told him that this would be a serious conversation. "What's up, Son?"

Daniel sighed loudly. He decided that the best way to begin this conversation was to simply blurt out the news. "Dad," Daniel's voice was earnest, "I want to marry her."

Peter Hatch kept his hands on the boat controls and remained very still for a moment. Even though he had anticipated having this conversation with his son for a long time, somehow he still didn't feel quite ready or prepared to. "You're only sixteen, Daniel. That's awfully young to be talking about marriage."

"Dad," Daniel's voice had taken on a logical tone, "I have known Meghan all my life." He felt like no further explanation was necessary. It was a solid fact that no one, including his father could dispute.

"I know, Son," Peter Hatch nodded thoughtfully, "but you're still only sixteen." He darted a pointed look at his son. "That's much too young."

"Dad," Daniel wasn't about to give up without a fight, "I want to get engaged to Meghan now. We won't get married until we've graduated from high school. That's two years away."

"That's still too young," Mr. Hatch mumbled as he squeezed the back of his neck. The tension within him was mounting. He could see that Daniel was very determined in this matter, and it would make it all the harder to dissuade him. At Daniel's age, he knew that a year or two seemed like an eternity.

"Dad," Daniel continued calmly, "how many people can say that they've known the person that they're going to get engaged to for sixteen years? Meghan and I go way back. We know each other very well."

"That's true, son." Mr. Hatch could feel his stomach ulcer acting up. "I don't have any problems with Meghan. The only reservation I have about the situation is your age. You're both too young. You have all of your life ahead of you." Mr. Hatch dropped an arm around his son's shoulders. "You know that I've always loved Meghan as if she were my own child. She's a wonderful girl. All I'm asking is that you wait a while."

"We'd only be getting engaged now," Daniel tried to keep his voice level and logical. "We would wait until graduation before we got married."

"Why don't you wait until high school graduation before you get engaged?"

Daniel sighed and ran a hand through his short black hair. "Dad, I feel like I've been waiting all my life to marry Meghan. She's the only girl I've ever dated and the only girl I've ever loved." Daniel sighed again. He wished he could make his father understand. "Getting engaged now is a compromise for me. I want to marry her now. Waiting two years to make her officially mine is going to seem like forever."

Mr. Hatch nodded understandingly. His son was so much like himself that it was easy for him to take his side. "I know, Son. Your feelings for Meg have been evident for a long, long time. Listen," he paused thoughtfully, "let me talk to your mom about this. We're going to pray about it for a week and," Mr. Hatch glanced at his son, "I want you to do the same. Pray about this for a week, Daniel, and really seek the Lord's will here. That's got to be more important than anything you desire." He sighed loudly. Maybe God would talk some sense into the boy. "At the end of the week, your mom and I will discuss this in depth with you."

"Thanks, Dad," Daniel tried to keep his enthusiasm down to a minimum. He felt a small victory that at least his dad had not come right out and said no. The answer he had given Daniel held promise. No matter how small that promise was, Daniel would cling to it like a lifeline.

"Dad," Daniel asked curiously, "didn't you and mom get engaged when you were pretty young?"

Mr. Hatch inwardly groaned. His past was about to come back and haunt him. "Yes," he answered slowly, "we did get engaged young at a young age."

"How young?" Daniel eagerly asked.

"Those were different times, Daniel." Mr. Hatch tried to successfully evade the question even though he knew deep down it wasn't going to work.

Daniel laughed. "You didn't answer my question, Dad. How old were you and mom when you got engaged?"

Mr. Hatch slanted Daniel a grin that soon blossomed into an all out smile. He knew Daniel very well and he knew his son would keep after him until he got an answer. "We were sixteen, Son. We had grown up on Lake Winnipesaukee, just like you and Meghan did. Your mom and I lived on islands that were so close to each other we could swim the distance. Just like you and Meg, your mom and I knew each other all our lives."

Daniel's grin was so wide that every tooth in his mouth was showing. "Wow," he shook his head, "that all sounds very familiar."

Daniel's tone was full of confidence. He felt like he was going to be granted the permission that he was so desperately seeking. After all, how could his parents say no to him after they had been in the same situation and done the very thing that he was trying to do. If anyone would understand, it would be them.

"I didn't say yes," Mr. Hatch warned quickly. "Those were different times, Daniel. A lot of kids my age got engaged while they were still in high school. It wasn't unusual at all."

Daniel nodded. "So," he asked smiling at his father curiously, "when did you and mom get married?"

Mr. Hatch sighed loudly. He knew that in answering his son's questions honestly, he would be giving Daniel the ammo he wanted to fuel his quest to marry young. He felt so torn up inside. "Son," he admitted quietly, "we got married right out of high school, two days after graduation."

Daniel grinned proudly. "That sounds like a great plan."

Mr. Hatch shook his head. "It sounds like a stupid plan. It was a very tough road, Son. I can't emphasis that enough. It's not a road that I'd recommend for two kids."

"Yeah, but you guys made it," Daniel shrugged casually, with only the naïve innocence that a young teen could have about a situation he'd fanaticized into thinking was rational reality. "When you love someone, you can get through anything."

"That's not true," Mr. Hatch couldn't hide his concern. Daniel wasn't going into this situation with his eyes open at all. "In my opinion, it's much better to wait. You can handle the stress that life throws at you much better when you're older."

"I love her, Dad. We can handle being married just like you and mom did."

"Daniel, that was a long time ago." Mr. Hatch knew that he was repeating his protests; he only hoped that some of the reality would sink in.

"Some things never change," Daniel dismissed his father's worries too quickly.

"Some things do change," Mr. Hatch's voice had grown heavy.

"Dad," Daniel turned to face his father, "you and mom have been happily married for all these years, haven't you?"

Mr. Hatch smiled at the thought of how much he loved his wife. "Yes, Son, I love her more than the day that I married her."

"See," Daniel looked lost in his fantasy of love, "we'll be just like that too."

"Daniel," Mr. Hatch warned, "many of the kids that got married right out of high school aren't happily married today. As a matter of fact, many of them are divorced. What your mother and I have is very special and unusual."

"What Meghan and I have is special and unusual too. Dad, I don't see the difference between your love towards mom and my love towards Meghan." Daniel sighed frustrated. "I don't see why we can't get engaged now."

"Do you want to know another reason why I don't want you to get engaged now?" Daniel nodded. "You're my son. I don't want to watch you take the hard road right out of high school." Mr. Hatch slowed the Sally G. as they neared Jerusalem Island. "I feel like the two of you would be setting yourselves up for failure. The odds would be against you, Daniel, and that's no way to go into a marriage."

"I feel like the odds would be for us," Daniel replied adamantly. "We have known each other all our lives. We have a special kind of love."

"I know, Son."

"Did grandpa like you getting engaged at sixteen?"

Mr. Hatch laughed loudly. "Not at all, and now I understand exactly how he felt."

"But he let you get engaged, didn't he?"

Mr. Hatch turned and looked at his son thoughtfully. "Yes, Daniel, he did."

Daniel grinned. "And you and mom are going to let Meghan and I get engaged, aren't you?"

Mr. Hatch sighed. He felt caught between a rock and a hard place. If he absolutely forbid Daniel and Meghan to marry out of high school, would he be forcing physical temptations on them that were too great for two young people in love to resist? After all, they had literally known each other all their lives and as far back as he could remember, they were in love with each other.

"Dad?" Daniel wasn't patient about waiting for an answer.

"Son," Mr. Hatch sighed again, "I said your mom and I would pray about it. Don't go picking out an engagement ring yet."

Daniel grinned shamelessly as he knelt to pick up the mailbag. "Dad, I picked a ring out for Meghan last year. I figured that I'd wait to bring the subject up until I finished paying for it."

"You finished paying for the ring?" Mr. Hatch asked in a voice filled with both alarm and shock. "You're kidding?"

Daniel shook his head and smiled. "I paid the last installment yesterday. I've given this decision a lot of thought."

"You should have discussed this with me Daniel."

"Did you discuss it with your father before you gave mom a ring?"

"No," Mr. Hatch whispered. "Enough for today, OK?" Peter Hatch felt too confused to continue this conversation. Daniel and Meghan were setting themselves up for a very difficult road, and he feared it would be nearly impossible to talk them out of it." He sighed. And when they turned eighteen, the law looked on them as adults. Legally, they could do whatever they wanted to anyway.

"You will talk to mom?" Daniel asked quietly.

"Definitely," he wasn't about to suffer through this alone, "and we'll get back to you in a week."

Daniel nodded and smiled excitedly. The expression on his father's face told him all he needed to know. By this time next week, he and Meghan would be engaged. He could hardly wait.

One

Meghan leaned against the white wooden railing and curiously watched the docks below. It was a Friday night and the waterfront at Weir's Beach was alive with activity. Behind her, the boardwalk was full of people. There were walkers, joggers, bikers, eaters, rollerbladers and the kids on skateboards that loved the challenge of swerving in and out of a large crowd.

There were parents pushing babies in baby carriages, some happy and some not as happy. Meghan smiled at a group of little girls that walked by with a mom. They all had pink balloons in one hand and pink cotton candy in the other. They looked very cute and very coordinated.

The smell of cheeseburgers and hotdogs drifted through the air, and as if on cue, Meg's stomach growled. You could get almost any type of food down at Weir's Beach. She laughed. Whatever was passing in front of her at the moment was the food she found herself craving. It all made her mouth water.

Meghan watched a little boy that looked to be around four years old pass by with his mom and dad.

He was holding a double decker chocolate ice cream cone with both of his chubby little hands wrapped tightly around it. He had a very determined look on his face as he carefully attacked his ice cream cone. Meghan smiled as she noticed he was not only wearing a cute blue sailor suit, but he was also wearing a good deal of his chocolate ice cream as well.

A scuffle on the north side of the dock drew Meghan's attention. Some tourist teenagers had pushed the mascot for the Taco House into the lake again. Jimmy Stewart, the local sheriff at Weir's Beach, was helping the costumed person out of the lake. Meg felt sorry for the mascot. Dressed as a large taco, the mascot roller-skated around the boardwalk trying to draw customers to the Taco House. At least once a week, a group of mean kids would grab the taco man by the arms and skate him into the lake. Meghan frowned at the sight. That was a job she would never do in a million years. She could think of many other ways to embarrass herself without doing that.

Meghan turned around and lazily looked about at the docks again. The docks were lined with almost every kind of boat imaginable. There were jet skis in every color, sailboats, both big and small, and of course, the ever popular powerboats. Meghan laughed at the thought of how her Aunt Birdie called powerboats stink boats. Aunt Birdie was a true sailor at heart. She couldn't imagine anything nicer than the quiet solitude of a sailboat as it noiselessly glided through the water.

As Meghan continued to watch the activity on the docks, she spotted Mr. Hatch working on his mail boat. He spied her at the same time and waved. Mr. Hatch was like a second father to her. The Hatch family lived on Pine Tree Island, which was only thirty feet from Cedar Island where Meg lived. She spent a lot of time with their family and felt more at home in the Hatch house than she did in her own house.

Meghan loved and respected Mr. Hatch. He was a strong Christian man and still happily married to his high school sweetheart for over twenty years. Mr. Hatch was always nice to everyone, whether they were a friend or stranger. His opinion of strangers was that they were simply friends that he hadn't had the pleasure of meeting yet.

Meghan smiled as she watched Capt. Hatch get his mail boat ready for the next day's deliveries. The Sally G. was a floating treasure on Lake Winnipesaukee. The boat was extremely popular with tourists and loved by locals as if it were their own.

As Meghan turned back to the boardwalk, she saw Daniel coming toward her. He smiled and waved at her and a moment later was at her side. "How's the most beautiful girl on the lake doing tonight?"

Meghan beamed. He always made her feel treasured. "Great now that you're here."

Daniel leaned over and kissed Meg softly on the cheek. " I love you," he whispered in her ear.

"I love you, too." She couldn't stop smiling. Every time she was around Daniel Hatch, she couldn't help but smile. He was everything that she had always dreamed of. Daniel was tall, dark haired and extremely handsome. He carried himself with a confidence that was well beyond his years. He was kind and gentle to all and sensitive in ways that she never thought a man could be. The little things in life counted with Daniel and he was so good at reminding her how much he loved her. He was a dream come true for her.

Daniel's face turned in the direction of the docks below. When he saw his dad, a quick smile spread across his face. "Hey, Dad," he shouted toward the Sally G., "do you need any help with your baby?"

Mr. Hatch laughed loudly. "No, Son, I'm just getting Sally ready for tomorrow's deliveries."

"Do you have a heavy load?"

"Yes," Mr. Hatch took his red handkerchief out of his back pocket and wiped his brow. "A family from Boston has bought the Bannister mansion and they'll be moving in tomorrow. I have a lot of boxes to deliver in the morning."

"If you want, I'll ride shotgun with you, Dad," Daniel's love for his father was clearly evident. "Maybe I can get some of the gang together and we can help you. It should make things go quite a bit faster."

"I'd appreciate that, Daniel," Mr. Hatch sounded very grateful. "Thank you."

As Mr. Hatch went back to work, Meghan slipped her fingers through Daniel's. "Do you ever look at your dad and feel like your seeing yourself twenty years down the road?"

Daniel smiled and nodded slowly. "All the time."

Daniel squeezed Meg's hand as they stood quietly watching the Mount Washington ferry slowly pull away from the dock. The Mount Washington was the largest ferry on the lake. It had four wide decks and boasted a passenger capacity of over a thousand. Every day they had a variety of entertainment to amuse their passengers and their dinner buffet was prepared by some of the finest chefs in all of New Hampshire.

As Meghan watched the passengers on the decks of the Mount Washington, a smile grew and slowly spread across her face. Some of the passengers were waving good-bye to people on the boardwalk; others had already started enjoying the buffet, while others were watching her as she watched them. She laughed and Daniel glanced at her curiously. "People watching is so much fun. There's never a dull moment."

Daniel grinned. "It's the best sport of all and I'd have to say, most of the time, very entertaining."

A loud, booming voice could be heard over the ferry's P.A. system. Daniel shook his head and laughed. "Capt. Jimmy is beginning his entertaining dialogue of the lake."

Meg smiled. "That man is so funny. Once he gets a mike in his hand, it's like his stand up comedian role begins."

Daniel laughed at a joke Capt. Jimmy was telling his passengers. "I'll tell you, Broadway is missing out on the biggest ham that ever lived."

They watched the ferry for a few more minutes as it's slowly made it way toward Rockport Harbor. Meg loved how the little white lights outlined the top of the ship. It made the Mount Washington look romantic and whimsical. More than one local had called the ferry the Love Boat and she could see why. It was a floating opportunity for many.

Daniel gently squeezed her hand. "I've got something for you."

Meghan loved the way Daniel's brown eyes twinkled when he was excited. "What?" she asked curiously. He was a master at giving good surprises.

Daniel's face grew thoughtful. "It's something that I've wanted to give you for a long time."

Meghan stared at her boyfriend. She was more than a little interested as to what he was up to. "How long?"

Daniel smiled lovingly. "A very, very long time." He paused as he dug into his blue cargo shorts. He pulled out a small plastic box and gently placed it in Meghan's hands. "It's only a token Meg. It's a promise of things to come."

Meghan's heart began to race. When a guy says that to you, marriage, white dresses, and diamond rings run through your mind. Meg opened the little box and gasped. A bubblegum machine, diamond engagement ring sat in the middle of a clump of cotton ball. Meghan's heart melted as she watched Daniel take the bubblegum ring and slide it on her engagement finger.

"Meghan," his voice had grown husky with emotion, "I'm going to get you a real engagement ring as soon as I've saved up enough money." Daniel's voice cracked and Meg felt the emotion of it strike her right in the heart. "I love you, Meghan. I always have and I always will." He gently turned her head slightly so their eyes met. "Will you marry me?"

The brilliant smile that covered Meghan's face answered the question before she could. In a voice filled with wonder, awe and excitement, Meg answered Daniel confidently. "Yes, Daniel, I will marry you. I love you."

Meghan couldn't stop smiling. She had always loved Daniel Hatch. She honestly couldn't remember a time when she hadn't loved him. They had grown up on Lake Winnipesaukee all their lives. They had played together since they were babies, yet as they grew up, a love that was special and deep grew between them. He was her childhood sweetheart, her Knight in Shining Armor, her trusted confidant and friend and now she was wearing his ring. Nothing could have made her happier.

Meghan looked down at the ring on her hand and smiled again. Even though Daniel had spent only a quarter on it, in her eyes it was priceless. It represented a life that was to come that they would share together. It represented love, hope and a promise of a happy life together. Someday a real diamond would replace this one, but this bubblegum ring would mean no less in her eyes.

"Meg," Daniel whispered, "look under the cotton ball."

As she slowly lifted the cotton ball, her mouth dropped open in shock. There, hidden under the cotton, was a beautiful sapphire ring. The small stone had two little diamonds on either side of it. It was gorgeous.

Meghan looked up at Daniel with questioning eyes. He grinned at her. "After carefully consideration, I didn't think the bubblegum ring would hold up very well. I liked the idea of giving it to you, but it's not very practical to wear everyday. I figure that the sapphire ring can be your engagement ring until I can get you a real diamond."

"It's absolutely stunning." Meghan felt like she was in a trance. Daniel slipped the bubblegum ring off her finger and slid the sapphire one on. "Save the bubblegum ring as a token and wear the sapphire one to let the world know that you are mine."

"Gladly," Meghan looked up into Daniel's big brown eyes. She felt so happy that she thought her heart would explode with joy. Life had been hard for her and her sister Lindy, but now things were turning around. From this point on she wouldn't look back at the past. She would keep her eyes focused straight ahead on the future. That's where the Promise Land lay for her.

Daniel leaned down and softly kissed Meg on the lips. "I love you," he whispered as he pulled back an inch from her lips. "I have always loved you."

"I love you too, Daniel," Meghan smiled. Her head was spinning. Today she was going from Cinderella to a true princess.

Daniel stepped back and held both of her hands in his. "I know that some people are going to say we're too young."

"Some will," Meg nodded thoughtfully.

"Not many people can say that they've known each other for sixteen years," Daniel grinned.

"Not many people can say that they've played with their future husband in a playpen either." Meg laughed. "We really do have some serious history going on between us. I don't know anyone, except for your parents and mine, that I've known as long as I've known you."

Daniel smiled. "Same here, honey. I'd like to get married right after we graduate from high school if that sounds OK to you."

"That sounds great."

"Then we can go off to college together," Daniel wrapped Meghan in his arms.

"That sounds good, too." She turned her head and smiled up at him. "I can see you've given this a lot of thought."

Daniel nodded. "I've been thinking about marrying you all my life. I'd say that's a lot of thought."

"Will you wait for me, Meg, until we graduate?" The hesitancy in Daniel's voice broke Meghan's heart

"Daniel," she hugged him hard, "I have waited for you all my life too. What's two more years?" Her eyes were tearing up. "I will wait for you forever."

Daniel wiped her tears away with his shirttail. "Hopefully we won't have to wait that long."

Meghan smiled. "I hope not, but I will Daniel. I love you so much."

"I love you too," he whispered right before he leaned down and kissed her again. Meghan was right for him. He hugged her harder. She was good for him and they had always been so perfect together. It was as though God himself had designed them just for each other.

He looked forward to becoming her husband and starting a family together. For now, Daniel touched the sapphire ring on her finger; it would have to do. Being engaged was the first step but being married was what he really wanted. Daniel sighed. He prayed that the next two years would pass quickly. He knew he wouldn't really be content until Meghan was at his side for good. He needed her like he'd never needed anyone. He sighed again. Two years was going to be too long. It was going to seem like forever; and in this case, forever couldn't come soon enough.

Two

The next morning, the whole gang showed up to help Mr. Hatch make his deliveries to Banister's mansion. Meghan's family owned and operated the Cedar Island Marina. Her job was piloting the water taxi to the many islands on the lake for the locals as well as the tourists. Meg's small ferry held only thirty passengers, but she figured it would be plenty big enough to carry several of Mr. Hatch's larger boxes.

Web came over to tie her dock lines as she pulled up to the town wharf. "How's it going, Meggie?" Web's eyes held a distinct mischievous glow to them. He loved to tease his friends, and she already knew what was coming her way. "Has anything interesting happened lately?" He stood grinning at her proudly, obviously knowing the answer to his own question.

Meghan couldn't help but laugh. Webster T. Long, Jr., was the biggest joker that Meghan knew. The way he teased his friends was almost an art. Meghan decided to tease her friend right back. "Lots of stuff has been happening, Web. The lake is a busy place."

Webster laughed loudly. "Uh huh," he stood there with his hands on his hips. "Are you going to pretend that the most exciting event of your life didn't happen last night?"

Before Meg could answer, Simon Kensington came over and helped her out of her boat. He quickly wrapped Meghan in a big hug. "Congratulations, Meg. I am so happy for you and Daniel. It's about time that the two of you have made it official."

"Thanks, Simon," Meg hugged her brotherly friend right back.

"Oh, coming through, coming through," Web shouted as he shoved Simon aside. "I was hoping you would tell me right away, Meggie," Web hugged his long time friend, "but you felt the need to torture me a bit." Web took a step back from Meghan. "I'm sure I've never done anything to you that deserves this type of treatment."

Both Simon and Meghan broke up laughing. "Web, don't go there with me. The list of what you've done to me personally is very long." Meghan grinned at him. "I don't forget, Web. Someday, I'm planning an incredible payback."

Web laughed. "I look forward to it with all my heart. I honestly do. But hey, enough about me, tell me about you. Were you totally shocked by the proposal or did you see it coming for a while?"

Meghan smiled. She knew she was glowing and she wasn't even about to attempt to hide it. To hide the love and excitement she felt inside would be impossible. "We have been dating for a long time, Web. I really wasn't too surprised."

"That's true," he nodded "but what I'd like to know is why in the world didn't you tell me when it happened?"

"We only got engaged last night, Web," Meghan smiled at her friend.

"Last night?" Web scratched his head. "This monumental event happened last night and you're just getting around to telling me now?" Web sighed dramatically. "No one tells me anything anymore. I feel so wounded. When did I get booted out of the gang? I've been kicked from first class to coach without even knowing it."

Meghan laughed and smacked Web in the arm. "You'll always be in the gang even if you exaggerate more than anyone I've ever known. Now, go help Mr. Hatch. I've got to check on some things on my boat. I'll be along in a minute."

"Yes, Ma'am," Web saluted her and walked toward the mail boat.

"We'll talk more later, Meg," Simon turned toward the Sally G., "I'm very happy for you."

"Thanks, Simon." As Meghan watched her friends, she smiled as she thought about how much they were really like family to her. Daniel Hatch, Webster T. Long, Jr., Simon Kensington and her little five-year-old sister Lindy had all grown up on Lake

Winnipesaukee all their lives. Even though their backgrounds were different, their bond of friendship was one of the strongest that Meghan had ever known.

Daniel, the love of her life, lived on Pine Tree Island with Web. Daniel had a strong Christian family with a mom and dad that loved him very much. Daniel had a younger sister Pam that Lindy often played with or fought with, depending on the topic or occasion.

Webster was Daniel's neighbor on the north. His father, Webster T. Long, Sr. operated the only limo service on the lake. Web was brought up by his father and overly doting grandmother. His mother had died when he was three, losing a year long battle with breast cancer.

Simon Kensington had the most glamorous and high society life of any sixteen-year-old kid on the lake. He lived in a huge mansion on Governor's Island. You could only afford to live on Governor's Island if you were extremely wealthy. The real estate was so hard to come by that wealth alone was simply not enough. You had to be well connected in the inner circle of the rich and famous to purchase property. The only way the common man ended up in Governor's Island was to serve the rich in various forms such as maids, cooks, butlers and other serviceable positions. It was an elite man world closed off to the ordinary little guy.

The Kensington name represented power, old money and worldwide fame. Simon's father was the very famous and well-publicized United States Senator from New Hampshire, Grant Kensington. His family came from a long line of old New Englanders that had been active in politics almost since the beginning of the country. The Kensington family political history proudly included one United States President, ten U.S. Senators, four U.S. Congressmen, two Foreign Ambassadors, eight Governors and scores of local representatives. There were always several Kensington's representing the various New England states in D.C. and Meghan felt fairly certain that there always would be.

The Kensington family name was practically an institution in itself. It was synonymous with fame, fortune and scores of flocking fans. People couldn't seem to get enough of them and they were always eager for any news update on what the media had long ago tagged as America's royal family. They were the closest thing to royalty in the United States and because of that they were followed wherever they went by bodyguards and crowds of adoring fans.

The Kensington's were loved, respected, and well-documented wherever they went. If a Kensington showed up at any occasion, it was sure to turn into the social event of the season and a complete media circus. The media loved to photograph the attractive family and took advantage of every opportunity to do so. A Kensington on the cover of any magazine or newspaper guaranteed huge sales.

Meg thought a moment about Simon's father. He was a very attractive man, in his early fifties and turned heads wherever he went. He carried himself with a majestic sense of style that put him in a grand class all his own. Any commoner would have been labeled pompous and snobby, but Grant Kensington somehow managed to spin his act into something that was nothing short of a confident, sophisticated elegance. He acted more regal than the British royal family themselves and Meg was quite certain that he could give nobility lessons to any royal anywhere in the world.

If anyone deserved an Oscar for his performance, it was Grant Kensington. He had the suave ability to charm, persuade and win over even his toughest opponents. Even the scandalous stories of his numerous, sordid affairs did little to discourage his popularity among his colleagues or the voters. He was a legend coming from an American legacy, and the people kept him up on his high pedestal regardless of his extra-curricular activities.

Meg's eyes narrowed. Simon was nothing like his father or his older brother Reid. Reid Kensington was the heir to his father's throne both in the political sense as well as the way he charmed women. Reid was fair haired and better looking than Simon. Many people often commented on how much Reid looked like Robert Redford. Meg could see it. The similarity was too strong for anyone, including Reid to deny.

Reid used his appearance and his charm to manipulate those around him and he did it quite successfully. He had girls chasing him practically from the cradle. He had mastered the art of charming, persuading, and controlling others for his own benefit when he was a youngster.

Meghan sighed. She didn't like Reid Kensington any more than she liked his slick father. She wasn't drawn into their fan club by their money, power, influence or fast-talking charming ways. She didn't trust either one of them and purposely distanced herself from both of them.

Simon, on the other hand, was a gem. He was a true and faithful friend. He never tried to be anything that he wasn't, and Meg was sure that using people for his own benefit would never even enter his mind. Simon was the most down to earth, easygoing person that Meghan knew. He stood by her side in times of trouble and always offered to help any way he could. His quiet presence was one of the most comforting things that Meg had ever known. He never over-powered you with opinions or advice. He was simply there, usually in the background, quietly offering his help. He was one in a million and Meg was very thankful for his friendship.

Just then a Frisbee hit against her legs and she looked up to see who had thrown it. Meghan quickly spotted a smiling Daniel coming toward her on the boardwalk. "I thought you might want that since Snacks chewed up the other one."

Snacks, who was Meghan and Lindy's English Springer Spaniel, had been at the front of the boat with Lindy. As soon as the dog saw the Frisbee, she took off for it like a flash. Meghan laughed. She was always surprised at how fast Snacks could move if she really wanted to. She was a rocket covered in brown and white fur.

Meghan quickly snatched the Frisbee off the ground seconds before Snack's soft white muzzle tried to latch onto it. "Snacks, no!" Meg commanded the fur ball. Snack's ears drooped down, and her big brown eyes looked incredible guilty just as she always did when she was caught in the act of a crime.

"Your dog will eat anything that's not nailed down," Daniel patted the sorry- looking pet.

Meghan laughed. "Hey, you've got to give her some credit. She's always willing to take a shot at the stuff that's nailed down too. She doesn't discriminate against texture, smell or the level of difficulty it is to try to get the object into her mouth. She works very hard to try to eat it all."

"Just as I thought. You don't even care if what you put in your mouth is edible. Maybe it's an afterthought for you but definitely not something you concern yourself with right away. You really are shameless, Snacks," Daniel scolded the dog who still hadn't taken her eyes off the Frisbee. "Have you no pride in yourself at all?"

Meghan laughed. "Are you kidding? Snacks is a dog that eats her way through the world. It's the highlight of her day. I have no doubt that she would up and leave me for a stale donut or a piece of old sandwich." Meg shrugged. "It's her life."

Daniel lifted one of Snack's long floppy ears and whispered into it. "She's got your number, Snacks. Watch out."

Daniel stood up and walked over to Meghan. "So, how have you been?" He leaned over and kissed her on the cheek.

"Great," Meghan smiled up at her handsome fiancée. Daniel was a big guy. He was as broad as a football player and stood over six feet tall. His brown hair cut stylishly short made him look intelligent and handsome, but it was his eyes that Meg couldn't resist. He had the warmest, kindest brown eyes that Meghan had ever seen. They looked like inviting pools of hot chocolate, and she found that she lost herself in his eyes time and time again.

Daniel slid his fingers through Meghan's and then squeezed her hand tight. "Thanks for letting us load up the taxi. It will save dad a lot of time."

"No problem," Meghan smiled as the air horn on the mail boat sounded. "I think your dad is ready to get going."

Daniel smiled and nodded. "Web and Simon will ride with him and I'll tag along with you and Lindy and Snacks."

As Meghan's water taxi followed Mr. Hatch's mail boat across the lake, she couldn't help but notice her sister. Lindy was standing in the front of the water taxi, pretending the red Frisbee that Daniel had given her was a steering wheel. She turned and talked to Snacks often, treating the dog as though it were her passenger.

"What's she doing now?" Daniel asked curiously.

Meghan laughed. A little humor was always the best way to deal with Lindy. "She's mad at me because I won't let her drive the boat, so she's pretending that she's driving the boat anyways."

Daniel grinned. "She keeps you on your toes, doesn't she?"

Meghan laughed again. "Only every minute of every day."

"It must be hard being both mom and sister to Lindy."

Meghan inwardly cringed at the mention of the word mother. It always reminded her of her own mom and it wasn't someone she liked being reminded of. Her mom was addicted to alcohol and drugs for as long as Meghan could remember. Her earlier childhood memories were filled with both verbal and physical abuse. Her parents fought constantly; and for some reason that Meg could never understand, she often became the victim of her mother's rage. She was small, unable to defend herself against an adult and available to be a punching bag for her mother. Her mother always took full advantage of it, and as she got older, she continued the abuse by burning her cigarettes into Meghan's armpits, back and rear end.

Meghan's father never hung around and watched the beatings. He always took off right after the fights. When he returned, he could see the marks of abuse on Meghan, yet he never did a thing to make them stop. Meg wasn't sure who she hated more, her mother for beating her or her father for not stopping it. It had taken years after her mother had left for the anger to begin to melt away toward her dad. She knew she still harbored so much resentment toward him. There was so much about him that she didn't understand. How anyone could allow a child to get beaten was one of them.

Somewhere around the time Lindy was born, Meghan had just turned eleven and knew it was time to start fighting back. She knew she couldn't stand by and watch her mother hit her baby sister. She would hide Lindy in the boathouse at the earliest signs that the abuse was coming. She didn't always have a warning, but when she did she learned to act quickly and take advantage of the time to hide Lindy and herself from their mother.

Then one day, when Lindy was just a few months old, her mother just up and left them. She gave no warning and didn't say good-bye, but Meghan knew what was happening. She didn't once try to stop her mother. She didn't cry or beg and plead with her to stay. There were no warm fuzzy feelings between them. As she saw her mother walk out the door for the last time, a great feeling of release washed over her, and she began to cry. The tears were not tears of sadness, they were tears of relief. If her mother was gone, she wouldn't ever have to fear being beaten again. Lindy would be safe. There would be no reason to hide. Safety would no longer be an illusion; it would actually become a reality.

"Meg," Daniel dropped an arm around her, "I didn't mean to dreg up the past for you."

Meghan forced a smile on her face. "It's OK, Daniel. My past is not some- thing I'm proud of. I try very hard to keep my past in my past. Once in a while it blindsides me, but I quickly try to shove in it in the past. I have a life now." She brushed away a tear that had seeped out of her eye. "I don't ever resent taking care of Lindy. She's all I have, and I love her more than anything."

"I'm glad you have her, Meg. You and Lindy deserve better."

Meghan smiled and held up her engagement ring. "We're getting better." She paused. "The only problem is that ever since Lindy could talk she has been telling anyone who would listen that she was going to marry you someday."

Daniel grinned. "She's been a fan for a long time."

"I don't think she really understands that wearing your ring means that I'm going to get you."

"I'll always take care of you both," Daniel's voice was full of love and compassion. "We are family. We take care of our own."

Meghan nodded feeling an intense need to change the subject. "Do you know anything about the family moving into Bannister's mansion?"

Daniel watched her closely for a second and then took the hint to change the subject. "No," he answered slowly, still feeling full of concern for Meghan and the past that tortured her so, "but one thing I am pretty sure of is that the people on the lake will always refer to the mansion as Bannister's mansion. That house has been called Bannister's mansion for a hundred years, and it will likely be called Bannister's mansion for the next hundred. Tradition is a hard thing for Yankees to change. We like routine and will stay in it as long as possible."

Meghan had to agree. "You're right. I never thought of it but that place will always be called Bannister's." She paused thoughtfully. "Well, one thing that I do know about the family is that they must be filthy rich. Bannister's mansion must have cost a bundle, because it is almost as big as a resort."

"That's true," Daniel absent-mindedly reached down and patted Snacks who suddenly showed up at his side because he had taken a stick of gum out of his pocket. "You're pathetic," Daniel whispered to the dog. "Go lie down." Snacks ignored the command and continued to stare at Daniel intently.

Meghan just laughed. "My best advice is to ignore her when she begs for food, especially if it's food like gum that she can't have anyway."

"I guess no one ever told you that staring at someone is rude," Daniel addressed the ever-attentive dog. "And look at me, "he laughed, "here I am talking to a dog. You know," he leaned in close to Snacks, "I know you know what I'm saying. Now go lie down." To his amazement, Snacks actually did lie down.

As Bannister's mansion came into view, Meghan wrinkled her nose at it and Daniel noticed it. "Did you get some water spray in your face?"

Meghan laughed. "No, I just forgot how much I never liked Bannister's mansion."

"How come you don't like it? It's big…" Daniel waved a hand in the air.

"Yeah," Meg agreed, "it's big and has one of the best locations on the lake, but it's so dark. It's not friendly looking or welcoming at all." Meghan's eyes scanned the house. The house was built with dark brick and dark shutters. Even the windows looked dark and unwelcoming. "It looks like an institution instead of a home."

As the boats pulled up to the dock, Lindy, who was still perched in the very front of the water taxi, screamed. "Meghan there's a naked lady!"

Meghan darted her eyes in the direction that Lindy was looking and was in such shock that she couldn't say anything for a moment. The girl sunning herself on Bannister's dock looked to be around sixteen or so. She was blonde and physically very beautiful but she was wearing such a skimpy, hot-pink bikini that Lindy was actually right. It looked like she was almost naked.

As Meghan starting coming to her senses, she immediately called Lindy back to her. She wanted Lindy as far away from this girl as possible but that wasn't going to happen. Lindy, who was more curious than a cat, decided quickly that she wanted to remain in her front-row seat. This was a show that she had never seen before and she wasn't about to give up her seat so easily.

As Meghan's boat docked, Lindy and the naked girl were almost face-to-face. "Why aren't you wearing any clothes?" Lindy asked the girl candidly. She had never been one to beat around the bush, and this time was no exception.

Meghan cringed inside, wanting to find a place to either hide or die. Lindy had no tact, no fear, and not a single shy bone in her entire five-year-old body. It was a lethal combination, especially for Meghan.

"Lindy," Meghan ordered, "get back here now." She prayed the little girl would listen, because she had no desire to get up close and personal with the naked girl.

Lindy ignored Meghan and not only remained in her box seat position, she repeated her question to the naked girl increasing volume. "Why aren't you wearing any clothes?"

Meghan sighed disgustedly and began to make her way to the front of the boat to pull her inquisitive little interviewer back. When Lindy took on the role of news reporter, it was difficult to break her of it.

"Your skin is very white," Lindy observed loudly.

As Meghan climbed over the boxes trying to get to the front of the boat to intercept Lindy, she heard

Mr. Hatch choke down his laughter and the other guys on the boat seemed suddenly very preoccupied with anything but the white skinned, naked girl. Everyone was very embarrassed by the sight except for the inquiring mind of Lindy and the naked girl herself.

Lindy continued her running examination and dialogue. "You have goose bumps all over you too." Lindy leaned in close to her. "Maybe you should put some clothe on. Then you wouldn't be so cold." It was obvious to those who knew Lindy that she thought she was being helpful. She had gone from an investigative reporter to Dear Abby in a matter of seconds. Meghan rolled her eyes. She knew Lindy well enough not to even hope that things didn't get any worse. The way Lindy's mouth and mind ran, things always got worse. It was inevitable.

Meghan lunged over a box and grabbed Lindy's hand. With a vise grip hold on her she attempted to pull the girl back. Just as she did, the naked girl herself seem to come to life. She lifted her head slightly, and stared at Meghan and Lindy for a second before speaking. Her annoyance was displayed clearly across her milky-white complexion. Meghan knew a welcoming speech was not coming.

"Who are you?" The naked girl was not only annoyed she was downright condescending and snobby. Why this surprised Meg she didn't know.

Her arrogant tone was completely lost on Lindy. The little girl perked right up. "I'm Lindy," she answered in a cheerful tone, "and this is my big sister Meghan," Lindy paused for only a brief second, "and you're not wearing any clothes."

The guys on the boat could not hold their laughter back any longer. At the sound of it the blonde girl turned her head toward them. "What are you doing here?" She was no less welcoming to them. Meghan had to smile. It wasn't her and Lindy that brought out the naked girl's temper, it was anyone who inconvenienced her and irritated her.

"We have a delivery. Are you one of the Bentleys?" Mr. Hatch asked, sounding remarkably like a man trying to hold back his own laughter.

"I'm Brittany Bentley," the girl stated as if that said it all. If she expected them to be impressed by her name alone, she would soon find out how disappointing that expectation was.

Mr. Hatch cleared his throat and nodded. "Good, these deliveries are for your family." Mr. Hatch paused and all eyes watched him. "Meghan," he added quickly, "please hand this clipboard to Miss Bentley. We don't want her to have to get up."

The light of understanding dawned on Meg instantly. No one wanted the picture in their heads of this near naked girl standing up. As Meghan handed the girl the clipboard and pen, she narrowed her eyes. How come everyone here was embarrassed but the naked girl? Lindy really didn't know better. She couldn't fault a five-year-old's curiosity, but this teenage girl knew better. What was wrong with her that she put on that outfit to begin with and then didn't die from embarrassment when the boats pulled up to her dock?

"Here," the girl shoved the clipboard back at Meghan. She dropped her head back down and sunk into her tanning coma again.

"She kind of looks like my Barbie doll without any clothes on." Lindy was more than fascinated.

As Meghan began dragging Lindy toward the back of the boat, Mr. Hatch called to her. "Meghan, we're going to move the boats to the end of the dock so that we don't disturb Miss Bentley any further.

Meghan almost let a nervous laugh slip out. She knew Mr. Hatch well enough to read between the lines. What he was really saying was, I don't want any of us around her. We'll unload at the end of the dock and ignore her.

When they were almost finished unloading the boxes, Brittany Bentley came to life. She wrapped a large white towel around herself and walked up beside Meghan's boat. She completely ignored Meghan and Lindy and zoomed her attention in on Daniel.

"Excuse me," she purred at him like a cat, "could you tell me what time it is?"

Lindy looked at the girl and then glanced back at Meghan. Before Meghan could slip a hand across Lindy's mouth, she spoke her mind. "Why are you asking him what time it is? You have a watch on. Is it broken?"

"Lindy," Meg hissed, "be quiet!"

Lindy turned around and Meghan knew the investigative reporter was at work again. "She's wearing a watch, Meghan. Why is she asking Daniel the time?"

"Oh," she hummed, "your name is Daniel. How nice. Do you have the time?"

Daniel stared at her face for a moment before answering. She was a snob and she was being snobby to his friends. That was a major mistake. "You've got a watch on. Look at it."

Meghan wanted to cheer. She was so proud of how Daniel had handled himself. The naked girl had a reaction that was quite different. Her mouth swung open and she looked utterly shocked. Meghan was pretty sure the rich blonde wasn't used to being turned down.

"I bet your warmer with that towel around you," Lindy chimed. Dear Abby was back. "You know, you'd stay a lot warmer if you wore clothes."

The girl stared hard at Lindy and then turned her heated eyes on Meghan. They held eye contact long enough to establish one clear fact. There was no doubt in either of their minds that they didn't like each other. Brittany Bentley was holding court and Meghan would eat dirt before she ever bowed down to her. She had never been anyone's fool and she didn't intend to start now.

"Do you go to school at Fenton Hall?" Brittany wasn't being nice. She was trying to get background information. Meghan almost laughed as it suddenly struck her that the rich blonde saw her as competition. She was a poor lake kid that lived on an island with no indoor plumbing. How could rich Brittany Bentley think of her as a threat?

Meghan watched Brittany's eyes skim over Daniel. Meg froze. Now she understood the game that Brittany from Boston was playing. She wasn't looking for information on Meghan; she was looking for information on Daniel. Her Daniel. She was openly checking him out, trying to decide if she wanted him.

Meghan cringed inwardly as Brittany's eyes narrowed. A sticky sweet smile spread across her face. She reminded Meg of the wicked stepmother in Cinderella. Brittany leaned close to Meghan, and whispered something that was intended for her ears only. "You know, Daniel is awfully cute." Meghan couldn't help but stiffen. "I believe it's not going to be so boring around here after all."

As she turned and walked away, Meghan felt a sense of dread flood over her that she hadn't felt since her mother left. Instinctively Meg knew she was no match for the beautiful rich girl from Boston. Brittany was playing a game that Meghan hadn't ever played before and didn't know the rules to. Brittany was trouble and somehow she knew she was going to get trampled by her. A sense of hopelessness filled Meghan as she suddenly realized the game had been played and was already over. Meghan had already lost without ever taking the court. It was over and so was the fairy tale in Meghan's life.

Three

Early Sunday morning, Meghan began her weekly rounds to pick up her church passengers. The majority of her customers were seniors who needed a ride to church because they no longer owned a boat. The rest of her crew was made up of families and tourists visiting the lake. There was never an empty seat on Meghan's taxi on Sunday mornings.

Alton Bay, located at the southern end of Lake Winnipesaukee, held a weekly Sunday church service at 9:00 A.M. The pastor would preach from the gazebo on the town green that was right on the waterfront. People came from all over the lake to hear the service. The majority of the crowd was boaters because you could dock your boat by the gazebo and stay in your boat for the entire service. The gazebo service was well attended each week.

Alton Bay Baptist Church would often have guest speakers and soloists perform at this service in the summer. An usher standing on the docks handed Meghan a bulletin, and she glanced at it. Today a pastor from California was speaking. She smiled as she watched the pastor come to the podium. The guest speakers always had a look of astonishment on their faces as they looked out over the sea of boats that came to listen to them. Meghan had to admit it was a unique sight. It wasn't every day that a preacher looked out over his congregation and had the audience sitting in boats. It probably did take a little getting used to.

A man from Canada was the guest soloist. As soon as he started singing Meghan knew there was going to be trouble. Lindy's mouth dropped open and the little girl turned in her seat towards Meg. An expression of utter astonishment covered Lindy's face. Meghan inwardly groaned. She knew she was about to have a showdown with Lindy because the man singing, quite honestly couldn't sing, and Lindy wasn't going to let it pass.

As the P.A. system carried his tuneless voice far and wide, Lindy leaned closer to her sister. "He can't sing," she stated too loudly.

"Quiet, Lindy," Meghan scolded the girl.

"Why is he singing when he doesn't know how to sing?" Lindy looked perplexed. "Doesn't he know that he sounds awful?"

Meghan slid a hand across Lindy's mouth. "Not another word. Do you hear me?" As Lindy stared at Meg evenly, it became instantly clear that the little music critic wasn't agreeing to anything. Meg knew it was time to throw the ultimate punishment down on her. "If you say another word about his singing, you'll get no dessert for a week." The passengers sitting around the sisters laughed, but Meghan continued to stare at Lindy threateningly. "Do you understand?"

Lindy reluctantly nodded her head. "Can we talk about this later?"

Meghan slowly nodded. "Yes, we can, but only at home and only to me. Do you understand?" Lindy nodded again, and Meghan cautiously removed her hand from her sister's mouth. With Lindy, Meg had learned that you could never be too careful.

Lindy changed gears quicker than a sports cars. "Are they going to ring the bell at the end of the service?"

Meghan sighed. Keeping up with her little sister's mind was a challenge at times. "They always do."

"I want to ring it," Lindy insisted.

"You know the story to this, Lindy. The pastor always gets to ring the bell."

"But I want to!" Lindy's voice was growing in volume.

Meghan stared at the girl as she put a first class pout on her face. "You're not getting anything with that pout. Erase it off now and maybe I'll talk to Pastor Joel and ask him if you can ring the bell one of these Sundays."

The pout disappeared immediately and was replaced by a glowing smile. "But," Meg whispered in her sister's ear, "you need to promise to be good. If you don't, I'm not going to speak to the pastor." Lindy frowned. It was obvious that she didn't like the strings attached to the deal. "Shake on it or I'm not going to ask him." Lindy shook Meg's hand but she didn't look happy about it.

"Now, be quiet for the rest of the service." Daniel Hatch, who was one boat away from Meghan's laughed. Meg leveled him with a hard look and he instantly mouthed the words sorry.

As Meghan began to focus on the pastor's words, her mind grew serious and thoughtful. His message was on trust, based on Proverbs 3. He encouraged the people to put their trust in God, not in people, not in money, not in things but in God and God alone. He told the people how God always took care of His children. Meghan smiled. She was living proof of that. God had taken care of her and Lindy and she knew that God would continue to do so in the future. Meghan sighed. That was why she trusted in God so much. He didn't disappoint her or let her down. He was the solid rock in her life that never crumbled. He was always there no matter what time it was or what the circumstances were. God was always there. The comfort of that thought brought tears to her eyes. God was the one person in her life that was always there.

Meghan almost began to cry when the pastor closed his sermon with Psalm 68:5. "A father to the fatherless and a defender of widows is God in His holy dwelling." This was one of God's promises that she repeated daily and clung to with all her strength. God would take care of her and Lindy. He promised to and she believed it with all her heart.

Just then Lindy turned around and Meghan knew by the confused expression on her face that a question was coming. "Is he talking about us?" Lindy whispered. Meghan nodded and brushed away another tear. Even though Lindy was only five, she understood. They had a father, even though he wasn't much of a father. He almost always had a beer in his hands and every evening, instead of tucking her and Lindy into bed, Bruce Kane would fall asleep in a drunken stupor, in his old beat up green recliner.

A troubled sighed escaped Meg. At least their father, as sorry as he was, was so much better than their mother. He never beat them or ever raised his hand to them. Even though he drowned himself in alcohol every night, they never felt threatened for their lives. It wasn't the perfect TV family, but it wasn't the nightmare that Meg had known either.

Meghan closed her eyes as the abusive images from her past flashed like pictures in her mind. It was not the typical family photo album. There was so much pain and heartache during that time. The only good thing that had come out of all those awful days was the birth of Lindy. She glanced at the little girl and smiled. As much as Lindy was a challenge in so many ways, Meghan knew she was the biggest blessing that she had been given.

After their mother had left, at eleven years of age Meghan had stepped up to the plate and become both mother and father to the baby girl. She had tried hard to do her best to raise Lindy. Lindy deserved better and deep down Meghan knew that she did too. Meg ran a hand through her long brown hair. Life wasn't fair but she never complained. Things could always get worse. She had lived through life when it was a lot worse and she never wanted to live through those times again.

Meghan smiled. God was taking care of her and Lindy despite life's hard knocks. Right after their mother had abandoned them, Aunt Birdie, her mother's older sister had come to live in the cottage right next door to them on Cedar Island. Meghan often felt that Aunt Birdie was an angel sent from God. She taught Meghan how to take care of Lindy and made sure the girls had food to eat and were loved. She knew that if it wasn't for Aunt Birdie that she and Lindy might never have made it. She was their guardian angel.

Meghan's thoughts drifted back to her father. Right after her mom had left her father started drinking. He had never drunk alcohol before but now he devoured it with a vengeance. He turned to the bottle for comfort and tried to drown out his intense loneliness and grief. Meghan wished her father knew God. She knew God would comfort him and take away his loneliness like nothing else could.

Meghan bit her lip to keep from crying. God was her rock to stand on and she knew God could be her dad's rock too if only he let Him. Maybe someday, that was always her hope and prayer.

The sound of the bell ringing jarred Meghan's thoughts back. The service was ending and she knew she hadn't heard half of it. All she could remember was that God was the father to the fatherless.

Lindy's quiet voice sounded in Meghan's ear. "Does that mean mothers too? We have a father but we don't have a mother. Does that mean that God is like our mother too?"

Meghan felt like she was going to choke on her tears. "It means that God is going to take care of us, Lindy. We don't have to worry or be afraid. God will always be with us."

"Aunt Birdie takes care of us, too," Lindy added thoughtfully.

Meghan smiled. "Yes, Honey, Aunt Birdie takes care of us too."

As Meghan started her water taxi, to return her passengers to their different islands, she smiled at the truth that she clung to. God had taken care of them and He would continue to do so even if they didn't have a mother or much of a father. They had God and Meghan had really learned at an early age that He was all she really needed. A mother and a father would be wonderful but God was God and He had stepped in to personally take care of them. The thought comforted her and overwhelmed her at the same time. God was good. He would take care of them and she knew she could rest in that promise.

Four

 $\mathcal{M}$ eghan and Daniel met at the dock that Mr. Hatch had built halfway between Cedar Island and Pine Tree Island. Since it was only a fifteen-foot swim for both of them, they met at the dock as often as life would allow.

As the moonlight shone down on them, they talked in a quiet whisper. "I can't believe your dad has increased your hours on the water taxi. I feel like I never get to see you anymore."

"I know," Meghan admitted frustrated. "Dad had to let go of Tom Benny who took the evening shift. I have to pick up his hours."

"Are things really that tight at the marina?"

The questioning tone of voice Daniel used made Meghan laugh. "Things have always been tight at Cedar Island Marina." Meg paused thoughtfully as she watched the moonlight shine out across the water. It made a beautiful golden path that looked inviting enough to walk on.

"Daniel, I didn't realize how bad things were until Dad laid the new schedule on me." She turned her head and looked at him. "I have to work. I have no choice in this."

Daniel exhaled loudly. "Why the change? What's happening at the marina?"

Meghan wondered how much of the truth she should tell Daniel. She wasn't sure how much he could handle; and once she told him, she knew he wasn't going to like it. As she had gotten older, she began to realize that her dad was an awful businessman who made one unwise business decision after another. When you combined the poor decisions with all the drinking that he did, it was a sure fire recipe for disaster. It was really a miracle that the marina was still running at all.

Meghan glanced casually at Daniel. She had been forced to grow up much faster than he had. He lived a charmed life with two parents that loved him, and he never had to worry about a financial decision in his life. One major difference between them was he knew that he had a next meal coming and a warm place to sleep. She did not have that same luxury. She never took the small things in life for granted. Most people thought that a warm house and three square meals a day were a God-given right being an American. Meghan had learned at an early age that it was not a right at all, it was a huge privilege.

She shook her head slightly. How do you explain to someone who's never gone hungry a day in his life what it's really like? How could he possibly understand the pain you get in your stomach when you don't have food? How could Daniel ever understand what it's like to be kept awake at night because you were so hungry or cold you couldn't sleep?

Since they had become engaged, Daniel had become very possessive of her time. He wanted to spend every minute of every waking hour together and that just wasn't possible. The hours that her father gave her took up most of her time. She knew that if she didn't work, she and Lindy wouldn't eat. It was that simple and basic for them. If you work, you will eat.

"Meg?" Daniel asked questioningly. "Have you gone off on me?"

Meghan nodded her head and laughed softly. She decided that since she couldn't think of a good way to explain things, she wouldn't. At least not right now. "I'm sorry I have to work so much but it won't be forever."

Daniel sighed. "It just seems like it will be. I get off work from the mail boat at four. You're still working every night until nine." Daniel exhaled loudly. "I don't like it."

Meghan felt her temper fire up. "That makes two of us Daniel. I don't like it either but I don't have a choice. I resent the fact that you make it sound like I do. If I don't work Daniel, Lindy and I won't eat."

He swung his head around and stared at her. "I'm not kidding. It's that tight. We've already gone without dinner five nights this past week."

Daniel's eyes widened. "Why on earth didn't you say something? You know you could have eaten with us."

"Daniel," Meghan laid a hand on his arm, "I'm picking up Tom Benny's hours. The extra hours mean more money. We should be fine."

Daniel didn't seem convinced but he was wise enough to let the subject drop. "Well," he blew the air into his cheeks for a second, "at least we still have the concert to look forward to. Saturday night is just a few days away."

Meghan swung her eyes away from Daniel and studied the dark water before her. "Meg?" Daniel questioned. "You're still going to the Michael W. Smith concert with me at Weir's Beach, aren't you?"

Meghan knew she was going to cry. She was being forced to make adult decisions when she was still only a child and she hated it. Life had robbed her so much of a normal childhood and now it was about to rob her again and there wasn't a thing she could do about it. "I have to work," she said in a voice that was barely audible. "Saturday is our busiest day."

"Meg," the disbelief in his voice cut through her like a knife, "we planned this six months ago. It's not like Michael W. Smith comes to Weir's Beach every

year. This is a big deal." He touched her shoulder
again. "Take Saturday off."

"I can't," Meghan's voice was strained.

Daniel stood up. "You have to. I already bought
the tickets. We planned to go with Simon and Web.
Please," he begged her, "take the night off."

"Daniel," Meghan stood up and faced him, "not
everyone has the freedom to make their own choices.
You seem to think everyone has that luxury. I never
did and I won't for several more years." Meghan
stared at Daniel's angry face in the moonlight. No
longer did the moon cast a romantic glow on the dock.
The light spread across the pine boards now looked
haunting and eerie.

Daniel threw his hands on his hips irritated. "If
we don't spend time together our relationship is
going to sink."

Meghan bit back the tears. She wasn't about to
let him see her fall apart when he was acting so self-
righteous. She knew what Daniel had just said was
true and she felt the anger rise within her as she knew
she was being robbed of yet another choice that she
didn't have the freedom to make. It wasn't the first
time in Meghan's life that she felt trapped and helpless and somehow she knew it wouldn't be the last.
As she watched Daniel dive into the black night
water, her hope went with him. The only thing left

facing her was a hard, unforgiving reality. It was a reality that no kid should have to face alone.

Once again her mind drifted to the sermon she had heard earlier that day. God was a helper to the fatherless...He was her rock and the only one in her life that had never disappointed her. He was always there and always understood the reason for all her tears. Life was tough but at least she had God. If she didn't, she knew that life would be downright impossible.

Five

Simon and Webster arrived at Cedar Island Marina bright and early the next day. As Lindy ran over to the docks to greet them, Snacks tagged along at her heals. Simon was eating a jelly donut and the dog was eyeing it eagerly.

"You know that I can't share this with you Snacks," Simon smiled at the ardent attention he was receiving from the Springer Spaniel. He pulled a doggie cookie from his pocket. "This should make you happy for about ten seconds."

Before Simon threw the cookie to the dog, he paused to read some writing on the front of it. He laughed and shook his head and Web asked what he was laughing at. "It says right here on the front of the dog cookie that it's tasty." Simon laughed loudly. "Well, how do they know that? The dogs don't talk and I seriously doubt they have human's testing canine food. I'd really like to know how they can claim this cookie is tasty."

"Snacks here looks happy enough." Web patted the cute dog's head.

"Yes," Simon grinned, "but she hasn't come right out and said that the cookie was tasty. I'd like to know their source. Who is it exactly that says this dog cookie is tasty and what right do they have to put it on the front of the cookie without identifying their source? It could be called false advertising."

"Man," Web scrunched his face up, "if you're thinking that I'm going to try to eat a dog cookie to verify their claims that it is tasty, you're nuts. The dog looks happy. Let's leave it at that."

"I guess we'll never really know then, will we?"

Webster laughed. "I don't know about you but I can live with that."

Meghan laughed as she went over her schedule for the day. She was listening to a typical Simon and Webster discussion. They always seemed to pick up on the little things in life that others overlooked. She laughed again. There was never a dull moment around either one of them. As she glanced at her morning schedule, she saw she would be making a variety of stops. Some people took the taxi from various pick up points around the lake, while other people called and scheduled their appointments.

Meghan turned the paper over and smiled as she saw her afternoon appointments. Miss Grace hosted a bridge club meeting for seniors every Monday afternoon. Meghan would pick up seniors from around the lake and deliver them to Evergreen Island where Miss

Grace lived. She enjoyed shuttling the seniors. They were a happy, lively group that always was fun to become a part of even if it was only for the ride.

"Hey, want some company this morning?" Web dropped an arm around her. "Simon and I are looking for something to do."

Meghan smiled. Simon and Web would often come along and keep her company when her schedule got crazy. She was grateful they would ride along with her, because she knew it would be the only time she'd get to see them. They were special friends, and she loved them like brothers.

"I'd love your company," Meghan smiled. "It makes my day pass much quicker when you guys are around."

"What's the schedule this morning, Captain?" Simon came up and offered Meghan a bag of M&M's.

She gladly accepted them. "Thanks, Simon. You spoil me."

Simon laughed. "I'm always glad to, Meg. You need a little spoiling. You work too hard." Simon paused and looked around. "Hey, I'm going off to the little boy's room. I'll be right back."

"Uh, Simon," Meghan couldn't hide her hesitancy, "you remember that Cedar Island has only outhouses for bathrooms, don't you?"

Simon's cheerful, easy-going expression dropped of his face. "Hey, big guy," Web came up and put a hand on his six foot tall friend, "how on earth could you forget a thing like that?"

"I don't know," Simon still remained expressionless. "Well," he shrugged his shoulders, "wish me luck, because I've got to do what I've got to do."

As he started marching off to the outhouse, Meghan called to him. "My first stop is at Weir's Beach. They have nice bathroom facilities there. Why don't you wait?"

Simon laughed. "That is no longer an option for me." He turned around and determinedly pushed himself toward the green outhouse building. Once he reached the door, he stood in front of it for a second, looking very indecisively about entering the small house.

"You'll be fine, Simon," Web coached his friend. "Just don't look down. If you do," Web laughed, "you'll never be able to go and you'll have nightmares about it for years."

Simon turned backed and looked at Web. "I thank you very much for your pointed and timely advice. I assure you, I'll take everything you've said into consideration." As he opened the door, they could hear Simon mutter, "A man's got to do what a man's got to do."

As Meghan and Webster howled with laughter, Simon stuck his head back out the door. "It's a two-seater." It was not a question but an unpleasant observation.

Meghan could tell that Simon was completely appalled. "Don't you have two seaters up in that big fancy mansion of yours?" Meghan and Web burst out laughing again.

"We don't even have one seaters," Simon laughed. "Give me a break. This is a completely new experience for me."

Webster grinned. "Yeah, we should be kind. It's easier upgrading yourself and much harder downgrading."

"I didn't know they made two seater outhouses." Simon was still in shock.

"Life is full of little surprises," Meghan laughed. "Would you like a magazine?"

"I don't believe I'll be here that long."

"Well, if you change your mind, just let me know. I'll send Web over with it." As Simon finally forced himself inside the little house, he could still hear Web and Meghan laughing.

"Man," Web shook his head, "what I wouldn't give for a camera right now. A picture of the wealthy senator's son coming out of a two-seater outhouse is priceless. I bet I'd be set for life."

"You're awful," Meghan swatted Webster's arm. "He's your friend."

"That he is but I'm also a businessman." Web wiggled his eyebrows up and down. "I know a business opportunity when I see one."

"You're awful."

"I know," he admitted proudly.

As they waited for Simon to emerge from the outhouse, old Mr. Pelley zoomed by them making a beeline for the outhouse building. He had his cane in one hand and his newspaper in the other. It was obvious that he didn't have any hesitations about using the outhouse and it was also clear that he intended to stay for a while.

"This is going to be trouble," Meg mumbled.

As Mr. Pelley determinedly pulled on the door handle of the outhouse, to his dismay, it didn't budge. His next plan of action was to bang on the door loudly with his cane.

"I'm in here," Simon's voice held the beginning sounds of alarm.

"Say something to Mr. Pelley," Web ordered. "This is your island and your outhouse."

As Meghan began to walk toward the agitated older man, Mr. Pelley began to shout at the green door. "Are you in there alone, young man?"

"Yes," the deflated tone in Simon's voice made in more than clear he wasn't happy about having a conversation through the outhouse door. "I'll be out in a minute."

"Now listen here, young man," Mr. Pelley's voice took on a commanding quality, "I happened to know for a fact that this outhouse is a two seater. I demand that you open this door at once!"

"No!" Simon sounded horrified. It was bad enough for the rich boy to have to use an island outhouse but the situation was about to escalate to an entirely different level if he had to become seatmates with old man Pelley. "I'll be right out."

"He's not going to be able to go with all this pressure," Web whispered to Meghan. "I know I wouldn't be able to perform my duty."

Mr. Pelley darted a look at Meghan. "It's a two seater. Tell the boy to open the door."

"He needs his privacy, Sir. Simon will be out in just a minute." Meghan prayed that Mr. Pelley wouldn't start banging on the door again. The situation was insufferable enough for poor Simon.

"I need to go in," Mr. Pelley stated emphatically. "I don't want to miss the taxi."

"I won't leave without you," Meghan assured him.

Just then, Simon flew out of the outhouse. As he passed Mr. Pelley, he gave him a hard stare. "It's all yours."

Mr. Pelley made a loud hump sound and then walked into the outhouse. "I'm leaving the door unlocked incase anyone else needs to come and use the other seat." He turned and looked at Simon. "That's the polite thing to do."

As the door shut behind the old man, Simon laughed. "You know, I really don't think it's so polite for him to leave that door unlocked. I'm not sure the sight of Mr. Pelley sitting on the outhouse toilet is a picture that's respectful to anyone."

Meghan and Web laughed. "Oh, do you have to use the outhouse?" Meg smiled at Web. "We'll be leaving soon."

Webster grinned back at her. "Not on your life, sister! I don't think I'll ever be able to go again. I'm going to live in fear of old man Pelley banging on the door. He's awful."

"He is kind of determined," Meghan laughed. "He's always been that way."

"I don't think he's determined," Web scowled. "What he did to Simon was downright rude."

As the three of them made their way to the water taxi, Meghan touched Simon's arm. "I'm sorry about that. Are you OK?"

"It was a most unpleasant experience," Simon sighed loudly. "Believe me, I won't forget it anytime too soon."

Webster laughed. "It could have been worse."

"In what way?" Simon asked "Mr. Pelley could have come in the outhouse and sat down next to you."

All three of them laughed. "That definitely would have been worse."

As Meghan made the trip from Cedar Island to Weir's Beach, her taxi had three customers in it plus Lindy, Simon and Web. Meghan almost laughed out loud as Simon noticed that two of the three passengers were Mr. and Mrs. Pelley.

"That's the boy from the outhouse that I told you about," Mr. Pelley pointed out none to quietly to his wife.

"Isn't that the Senator's son?" Mrs. Pelley was the nosiest person that Meghan had ever met. She enjoyed sticking her nose into other people business like it was some sort of hobby.

Meg glanced at Simon. She could just picture him rolling his brown eyes behind his sunglasses. Poor Simon. Being the Senator's son had few perks and more hassles than it was worth. On top of that, he practically had no identity outside his famous father's. Almost everyone referred to him as the Senator's son as though it were his name. Meghan felt sorry for Simon. He walked in his father's shadow and that was a difficult place for a kid to grow up in. She wouldn't trade her small island home or her outhouse for anything in his life.

As the taxi rounded the corner of Cedar Island, the Christmas Islands came into view. Bethlehem was the most populated. They even had their own store and church. Nazareth was on the right of Bethlehem and Galilee was on the left. Meghan smiled. She loved all the little islands on the lake. They each had their own special features, unique qualities and personalities of their own. Meg loved to explore them whenever she got a chance.

Simon, who was sitting next to her in the back of the boat glanced at her as he lowered his sunglasses. "What's she doing now?"

Meghan followed his eyes to where Lindy was at the front of the boat. She had to laugh. Lindy had her reserved seat in the very front of the boat. "She has decided to dress up as Queen Elizabeth today."

"Why?" Simon looked confused.

Meghan laughed. "Why not?" Lindy loved to play dress up and it was a rare day that she didn't put herself in some sort of costume. Meghan glanced at Lindy again and laughed. Lindy was standing in the front of the boat, wearing a dress that was five sizes too big on her. She was accessorized in an overabundance of costume jewelry. She had on three pearl necklaces, two bracelets on each wrist, clip on pearl earring and a gold crown that Meg had found at a yard sale. In one hand she had a royal scepter and in the other hand she had a huge black pocketbook that Aunt Birdie had given her. Queen Elizabeth, aka, Lindy Kane, stood ramrod-straight waving her scepter at each passing boat. It was a royal affair that only Lindy could pull off.

"I believe she's inspecting her kingdom," Webster observed seriously. "She actually looks quite good. The crown and the scepter really add a nice touch."

"Can't you discourage her from dressing up?" Simon didn't seem to appreciate the fact that he was riding with her royal highness.

"Are you kidding?" Meghan looked at Simon as if he were crazy. "Do you know how hard it is for me to talk Lindy out of anything? She's unbelievably determined once she sets her mind to something. Besides," Meghan glanced toward her little sister again, "today's outfit is actually less embarrassing than some other's she has. You should be grateful. Some days she wears the kitchen colander on her head as if it were an army hat. This is nothing."

"Well, I like it," Web smiled. "If she keeps the queen thing going I may have to join her at the front of the boats as the king."

Meghan shook her head. "That wouldn't work Web. Lindy likes to work alone. If you were going to join her in any capacity she would probably turn you into her servant. She wouldn't want you to out rank her."

"So she'd demote me?"

Meghan laughed. "Definitely. Remember we're talking about Lindy here."

Web frowned. "Well then forget that idea. I don't want to spend my day being bossed around by a five-year-old."

"She would too," Meghan laughed.

"I know she would. You see, if I were king, I could threatened to throw her in my dungeon."

"Your partnership with Lindy wouldn't last very long. She wouldn't be big on being thrown in anyone's dungeon."

Meghan smiled as Lindy saluted little Bug Lighthouse as they passed it. It was the only lighthouse on the lake and stood proudly on a large hill, overlooking the lake, with pine trees and evergreens standing gracefully behind it. The Bug Lighthouse was the smallest lighthouse that Meg had ever seen and this fact only made it appear cuter. It had all the bells and whistles that a regular lighthouse had but just sized down.

Bug Lighthouse was attached to a small lighthouse keeper's cottage. The small lighthouse was owned by the State of New Hampshire and could be rented out. It was especially popular with youth groups and school groups. When the lighthouse was unoccupied, Meghan and Lindy would often stop in and eat their lunch on the lighthouse keeper's porch as they watched the boat traffic on the lake below. Meg often stopped in by herself when she needed a bit of solitude. It was a private, relaxing spot to visit. Like the Sally G., Bug Lighthouse was another treasure on Lake Winnipesaukee that many of the locals claimed as their own.

As they continued down the huge lake, Meghan spotted the U.S. Mail Boat. The Sally G. was making a delivery at No Name Island. Lindy spotted the mail boat too. She lost her royal airs for a moment and began waving her hands frantically to get Mr. Hatch to blow the boat's air horn. She succeeded and a moment later the loud horn on the Sally G. blasted. Lindy smiled, stopped her waving and went back to her royal routine.

Meghan saw Daniel outside on the boat's deck. They waved to each other yet his serious expression made the greeting anything but friendly. Web and Simon had also noticed it and turned to Meghan with questioning eyes. "Is everything OK in Loveland, Meg?" Simon asked quietly.

"Fine," Meghan responded with finality in her voice that made it clear that the subject was not open for discussion.

Web leaned in closer. "It doesn't look fine to me."

"You're always trying to turn nothing into something," Meghan shot an angry look at Web. "Stay out of it."

"Is there something to stay out of Meg?" Web asked gently. "I'm only wondering about the cold shoulder Daniel just gave you. Maybe my observations are wrong."

"Observations can be wrong." Meghan stared off across the lake for a moment. The fact that Daniel was still mad was not a good sign. The fact that she couldn't do anything about it didn't help.

"Are we wrong?" The concern in Simon's voice broke Meghan's heart. He was always so kind and gentle and far too observant. Simon was never one you could fool about anything. He was far too perceptive for a kid.

"No," Meghan mumbled, "well, yes, I mean, oh," she sighed loudly, " I don't know."

"Were friends here, Meghan. Spill it," Simon encouraged her in his own quiet but persuasive style.

"You know that if you don't tell us, Daniel will. Whenever he's mad about something he always dumps it on us."

Meghan knew that Web was right. They would find out sooner or later. Web, Simon and Daniel were like the Three Musketeers. They were closer than close. Meghan sighed. "You didn't hear this from me, OK?"

"We know how to stay quite, Meg," Simon assured her.

Meghan nodded. "Daniel is upset with me because my father has increased my hours on the water taxi. I'll be working every day until nine at night."

"You have got to be kidding?" Simon asked. Meghan shook her head.

"What happened to Tom Benny?" Web scrunched his brow thoughtfully. "I thought he took the evening route."

"Dad had to let Tom Benny go." Meghan bit her lip to keep from crying. "Things are kind of tight right now."

"I'm so sorry Meghan," Simon dropped an arm around her shoulder and gave her a loving squeeze. "I wish there was something that I could do."

"Would your dad let me take some of your routes?" Meghan knew that Web's request was sincere but impossible.

Meghan sadly shook her head. "No, I'm sure he wouldn't." She turned to Web. "Thanks anyway. I appreciate the offer."

"Well, look on the bright side," Web had a forced cheerfulness in his voice, "at least you'll be able to go to the concert on Saturday at Weir's Beach. Michael W. Smith is going to be awesome in concert. That's something you can look forward to."

It was not the first time that day that Meghan felt like she was going to cry. Her throat tightened up and for a moment she couldn't speak. She just shook her head no.

"What?" Web leaned in close to her.

"I have to work that night." Meghan whispered at her feet. Life just wasn't fair at times.

"Meghan, I'm so sorry." Simon dropped an arm around her and she wanted to fall into his arms and cry. Instead, she took the quick hug that her friend was offering and bit her lip harder so she wouldn't cry.

"You know I can loan you the money," Simon whispered for her ears only.

Meghan looked at up at her friend with her eyes glistening in tears. "That's so nice of you, Simon, but my father would have my head if I took money from you or anyone else. He has a lot of pride about his business."

"The offer is always on the table, Meg. Anytime you need help, I'm here for you."

"Thanks, Simon. You're so sweet." They stared at each other for a moment and Meghan wondered for the hundredth time why she couldn't fall in love with Simon Kensington. He was the nicest guy she'd ever met and would make some girl a wonderful husband and father someday. "Thanks," she whispered sincerely.

"Anytime," Simon smiled and then broke the eye contact. "You're in a tight spot, Meg," Simon continued as he gazed out across the lake. "You have to do what your dad says but it's not giving you and Daniel much time together. That's hard on both of you."

"I just wished Daniel would realize that I honestly don't have a choice about my hours on the water taxi."

Simon nodded understandingly. "Oh, I think he understands, Meghan. What's tough for him is that you are a beautiful girl and he doesn't get to see you often enough. If I were in his place, I'd probably feel the same way."

Meghan punched Simon softly in the shoulder. "You always did know how to give a compliment, Simon. Thanks." Simon smiled gently at her and then went back to looking out across the water.

"You know," Web began thoughtfully, "this is the exact reason that I refuse to enter into any kind of romantic relationship at sixteen." Web turned and looked at Meghan. "No offense to you and Daniel."

Meghan laughed. "None taken, Web."

"Good," he nodded. "I just know that for me personally, I'm not ready for girls in that way. I don't plan to have a relationship that is any more than a friendship for a long, long time."

Simon laughed. "So, you plan on putting it off indefinitely?"

Webster laughed. "For as long as it is humanly possible. I may be a senior citizen before I'm ready." He paused and looked at Meghan. "I've always been a late bloomer."

Meghan and Simon laughed. "You don't always have a choice, Web." Meg looked at her friend with amusement. "When you meet the right girl, she's going to sweep you off of your feet whether you're sixteen or sixty." Meghan sighed. "I honestly can't remember a time when Daniel didn't sweep me off my feet."

"Yeah, you two were definitely meant to be." Simon lowered his glasses and winked at Meghan.

Webster closed his eyes and leaned his head back. "You see, that's what I mean. Even the talk of someone sweeping me off my feet simply scares me to death. I'm a late bloomer, and I'm not getting involved with any girls for another twenty years or so." He opened his eyes and stared at Meghan. "No girls," he said adamantly.

Meghan laughed and then turned a curious eye toward Simon. "What about you Simon? Is there someone that you like?"

Simon waved a hand at her and laughed. "If you're talking girls, that's Reid's department. I think I'm like Web. I'm a late bloomer too."

Web pointed a hand at Simon. "You and me brother, we're going to ride this chick thing out together. If we help each other, we'll get through this OK. You know," Webster paused thoughtfully, "Reid always does have a flock of girls following him around."

Simon laughed. "He always has. Better him than me," Simon laughed again. "So many of his fans are in love with his looks, or his reputation or his family status. He often feels frustrated that people don't know the real Reid. I feel sorry for him."

Meghan laughed. "I don't think I'd go all the way to sorry. You've got to admit, the way Reid flirts with girls, it's like he's got it down to a science. The Perfect Prince earns his reputation as far as I can see. He's the total package of tall, blonde and handsome and he uses the package every time he's with a girl."

Simon laughed. "That's true. He knows how to make things work for him. I'm tall, shaggy and dark haired. I feel like the total opposite of Reid. I never know what to say around girls. They terrify me more than anything. Well," he back pedaled, "except for you, Meg. You're not like the rest."

Meghan laughed. "That's good, Simon, because I don't want you to be afraid of me. Besides," Meg smiled at her long time friend, "you seriously under-rate yourself. I think you're handsome, smart and have the kindest heart I know. You're priceless Simon. Don't ever let anyone make you feel second class."

"Thanks for the vote of confidence, Meghan. Daniel Hatch has no idea how lucky he is." Simon grinned at her. "If he doesn't treat you right, you come find me. I'll always be here for you."

Simon's message was coming through loud and clear, and Meghan wondered what in the world was wrong with her that she didn't take him up on his offer. He was a great guy and she wished she could fall madly in love with him; but she knew love was something that you couldn't force. Meghan sighed. She would never lead Simon on or hurt him in any way. She'd have to be very careful about how she acted around him. For the life of her she wouldn't ever want to hurt this tenderhearted guy.

"You know," Web broke the awkward silence, "I think it's stupid the way girls follow Reid around. I think if they ever took a closer look at you Simon, they'd leave Reid in a second and be at your side forever."

Simon shook his head. "That's not what I want. I don't want tons of girls following me around. The thought of it scares me to death. All I want, down the road, is to find the right girl, just one," he laughed, "and marry her and have a bunch of kids. That would make me more happy than anything."

Web didn't miss the tender way Simon glanced at Meghan. He had had a serious crush on Meg for most of his life. Meghan never knew how deeply Simon cared. She didn't see it when they were kids and she didn't see it now. She always thought Simon cared for her like a sister but his feelings always went much deeper than that. Webster closed his eyes. It was just one more reason to stay away from girls. He didn't need the heartache.

"I will never fall in love," Web muttered loud enough for Simon and Meghan to hear.

Meghan narrowed her eyes at him. "You know what I think?"

Web laughed. "I don't think I want to know what you think but I have the unpleasant feeling that you're going to tell me anyway. Am I right?"

Meghan and Simon laughed. "Yes you are! I think," Meg paused momentarily, "that when you fall in love, you're going to fall fast and hard."

"Woman," Web mocked her, "that just goes to show you how little you know about me. I'm tough like a rock. I'll never fall in love."

"Those are famous last words..." Simon grinned. "She's right. You're not even going to know what's hit you. Be careful my friend."

"You two know nothing," Web dismissed them both.

As they rounded the corner of Indian Island, Meghan slowed her boat when the town dock came into sight. The dock was a large pine dock that had a typical green and white mailbox house on the far corner of it.

"What's up?" Web asked curiously.

"I'm scheduled to pick someone up," Meghan glanced at her route sheet.

"Who?" Simon asked curiously.

"A new family has moved onto Indian Island. I'm to pick up a lady named Natasha North. I'm supposed to take her to Weir's Beach."

"I don't see anyone on the dock," Web glanced around.

Right at that moment, as if on cue, a beautiful African American teenage girl came out of the mailbox house. She looked to be around sixteen or so. Meghan thought she was one of the most beautiful

girls that she had ever seen. She could have easily
been a model in one of those trendy magazines. She
even knew how to carry herself with style and class.

"Thanks for the ride," she smiled at Meghan as
she took a seat on the taxi. "We're new here and my
dad's been having trouble with our boat."

"You must be Natasha. I'm Meghan Kane. My
dad owns the Cedar Island Marina. If you're having trouble with your boat, I'm sure he could help
you. He can fix almost anything."

"Thanks," Natasha glanced at the other passengers aboard the boat. "I'll tell my dad. I think he's
going to need some help. He's not very mechanical."

Meghan quickly made the introductions of the others aboard the boat. "The queen at the front of the
boat is my sister Lindy."

"She's cute," Natasha smiled at the little girl.

"Sometimes…" Meghan mumbled. "This is Simon
on my right and Webster on my left."

Simon extended his greetings immediately but
Web sat there staring at Natasha as if she had three
heads. Meghan couldn't help but smiled. It looked
like her prediction about Webster's love life might
be coming true sooner than even she had anticipated. You never really did know when Cupid was
going to strike.

"Web," Meghan whispered, "don't stare at
Natasha like that. You're going to make her feel

uncomfortable." Webster immediately dropped his gaze to the floor.

Meghan smiled at Simon and Natasha and then just shrugged. As she glanced back at Web, he was so nervous that his hands were actually shaking. She pitied him. If he didn't get used to Natasha soon, it was going to be a very long summer for him. She smiled again. It was turning out to be quite a romantic summer sizzler. Now, she cast a quick glance at Simon, if she could only find someone for him. She'd have to pray about that. There were not to many girls around that deserved a guy like Simon.

As Meghan pulled up to the main dock at Weir's Beach, Lindy's high-pitched voice shattered her romantic notions. "Meghan, it's the naked girl! She's wearing clothes now so I bet she's warmer." As Meg's eyes went in the direction that Lindy was looking, a cold chill ran up her spine. She barely noticed the passenger's getting off the boat. Her attention was completely focused in on Brittany Bentley and Daniel Hatch. Even from a distance, Meghan could see that Brittany was flirting with Daniel. Her coy smiles, the way she quickly touched his arm and her piercing laugh as it cut through the air were nauseating to Meghan.

As Meghan continued to watch Brittany at work, flirting with her fiancé, she cringed as she took in her outfit. Brittany was decked out in an ultra tight hot pink spandex shirt that came down to the middle of her chest. Her short white mini skirt was so short that it was barely covering the essentials. Meghan shook her head. She knew what she was seeing but she couldn't believe it.

"It's probably not what you think," Web leaned close to her.

Meghan turned and stared at Web for a minute. "If it's not what I think it is then can you please tell me why he's just standing there letting Brittany drool all over him. He's not even trying to stop her flirting." Meghan glanced over at Daniel again. "You know," her voice was filled with pure shock, "it looks like he's actually enjoying all her attention."

"Meghan," Simon stared at the scene in front of him, "I'm sure Daniel has an explanation for what's going on."

Meghan's voice dropped low. "I can't wait to hear it."

"I'm sure it's going to be good," Web tried to reassure her.

"Web, from what I've just seen, it had better be more than just good. I can't wait to hear Daniel explain this."

"Me too," Simon's jaw was clenched together tightly. "You're not the only one that needs an explanation. I just don't get it."

Meghan shook her head. "That makes two of us Simon."

"Man," Mr. Pelley said loudly to his wife, "that girl talking to the Hatch boy has really big…" he suddenly seemed embarrassed, "uh, hair."

His wife slapped him in the arm. "Walter Pelley, you take your cotton picking eyes off her big hair." She sighed disgustedly. "For someone who claims they can't see well, you certainly see an awful lot."

Meghan groaned. Mr. Pelley was right. Not only was Brittany Bentley more gorgeous than a Barbie Doll, she was rich, better endowed than most women and knew how to strut her stuff to get all kinds of male attention. She was shameless but so were the men that gawked at her and right now that list of gawking men included Daniel Hatch. Meghan sighed. Her Daniel Hatch. What was he doing? She had never seen Daniel act like this before; then again, she had never seen a real live Barbie Doll throwing herself at him either.

As a high-pitched giggle drifted through the air, Meghan thought she was going to be physically sick. She glanced at the sapphire engagement ring that Daniel had given her. It didn't seem to have the same sparkle and shine as before.

As she looked back at Daniel and Brittany, it was perfectly clear that Daniel wasn't discouraging her advances. In fact, it appeared that he was welcoming them.

As the passengers at Weir's Beach boarded the taxi, Meghan shut her eyes for a minute trying to block out the nightmare that was before her. Her world was suddenly spinning out of control. Daniel, a person she had trusted and loved since childhood was changing right before her eyes. How could that happen? He had always been so focused and dependable and now it was like she was seeing a different person altogether. He had gone from being her best friend to a complete stranger.

As Meghan opened her eyes, she looked down at her ring again. It wasn't her fault that her father had changed the schedule and she had to work more. She wanted to see Daniel as much as she could. A thought suddenly hit Meghan so hard it literally left her breathless. Daniel didn't want to see her. If he did, he could be riding the water taxi with her on his off hours like Simon and Web did; but for some reason, that she hadn't yet figured out, he chose not to.

As she looked over at Daniel and Brittany again, she saw clearly what Daniel did choose. He wanted a real life Barbie Doll that was rich and had big hair that fawned and fussed over him like a mother hen. Meghan sighed. That would never be her and she never wanted it to be her. Meghan quietly slipped the sapphire ring off her finger. Not only was the engagement broken, so was her heart.

Six

$\mathscr{T}$he next few weeks passed in a blur for Meghan. Summer was falling into a predictable schedule, and Meg found a certain amount of comfort in the routine. The most important part of her routine was avoiding Daniel Hatch. She soon found that she didn't have to work very hard at it. Disappointment ripped through her as she realized how mutual the feeling was. Daniel seemed to be avoiding her as much as she was avoiding him. It seemed like the one thing that they agreed on these days was to avoid each other at all costs. Meghan sighed. Where had the fairy tale gone? How could something so right suddenly go so wrong? Within a few days of being engaged, she had managed to go from feeling like a princess to an ugly, unwanted pauper. The fact that Daniel had tossed her away for a Barbie Doll like Brittany did little to help her self esteem. It was something that she knew she would think about for a long time and wasn't convinced that she'd ever figure out.

Meghan studied her taxi schedule. Sundays she picked up the seniors for church, and Wednesday she picked them up for prayer meeting. Mondays and Thursdays she picked up the seniors to play card games. The other days of the week were divided up in servicing the different towns and villages around the big lake.

Life was full but one good thing that had happened was that her father had hired Tom Benny back part time. He covered four evenings a week so now Meghan only had to work three nights.

Meghan enjoyed the free time but the lack of income was starting to hurt them. She knew she was going to have to pick up another part time job. Things had gotten so tight at the marina that meals were short and often times dinner was skipped altogether unless Aunt Birdie happened to bring a meal.

As Aunt Birdie had grown older she became less aware of the needs around the marina. She didn't seem to be aware of how tight the finances were and that meals were once again being skipped. Meghan thoughtfully chewed on her fingernail. Aunt Birdie had done a super job to pull them through when she was a kid. Now that she was old enough to fill in the gap, all she needed to do was figure out another job that she could do that didn't have the same schedule as the taxi.

The very next day Meg started looking for work down at Weir's Beach. There was always a restaurant or business that needed workers on the boardwalk. She could waitress, sell tee shirts and souvenirs, or even work aboard one of the many ferries. She felt quite confident that she would find something.

As Meg scanned the storefront windows for help wanted signs, one ad caught her eye. The Taco House needed a waitress. She had known Mr. Santos, the man that ran the Taco House for years. She felt certain that he would at least consider her for the position.

As she entered the small Mexican-styled restaurant, Mr. Santos spotted her right away. "Well, hello there Meghan Kane. What brings you into my fine establishment this early in the morning?"

Meghan smiled at the middle-aged man. Mr. Santos was always so happy he could be labeled down right jolly. He would be a fun person to work around. "I saw the sign in your window that said you needed help. I can waitress and I can work three evenings a week."

The jolly look evaporated off his face. Meghan knew that was not a good sign. She braced herself for the bad news that was sure to follow. "Oh, Meg, I filled that position last night. I wish I knew you were available. I would have loved to have you work for me."

Meghan tried to hide her disappointment. "Well," she shrugged, trying to play it casually, "let me know if you hear of any job opportunities on the boardwalk. I need to pick something up right away."

Mr. Santos looked thoughtfully at Meghan. "You should go see Mr. Hatch. I hear he's looking for some help aboard the Sally G. That would be right up your alley."

"Daniel works with him," Meghan looked confused. Why would Mr. Hatch need help? He had his son.

"I don't know the details Meg, but I hear that he's looking for help."

Meghan didn't hesitate. "That wouldn't work out. I need something different."

Mr. Santos scratched his head. "Do you know how to roller skate?"

"Sure but…"she stopped in mid sentence as her eyes caught sight of something in Mr. Santo's office. The Taco man costume was dripping from a hanger. Someone must have just been jet propelled into the lake.

As she looked back at Mr. Santos, he smiled. "What do you think?"

"Oh, no way." Meghan instinctively started backing up toward the door. "I'm not the person for that job."

"It pays ten dollars an hour, Meg, and all you have to do is skate around the boardwalk. It could be a fun way to pass the evening."

Meghan shook her head. She desperately needed the money, but her pride wouldn't allow her to reduce herself into being Taco man. Taco man was always targeted by mean kids and ended up getting tossed into the lake at least once a week. No amount of money was worth that type of humiliation. She'd rather starve to death.

"I'm going to keep looking," Meghan said to Mr. Santos as she walked out the door. There had to be something better. Anything. Anything was better than Taco man.

As Meghan made her way down the boardwalk, she began to pray and ask God to help her find a job. She should have prayed earlier about it. Maybe then she wouldn't have been faced with the Taco man decision. She knew that God had something for her that didn't include humiliating herself on a regular basis.

As she began to pass the local newspaper office, The Lake Winnipesaukee, she decided to go in. She could pick up a paper and find out about the jobs available.

"Meghan, what brings you in here this morning?" Mr. Nak was the manager of the Lake Winnipesaukee. He was tall, thin and in his early sixties. He had short dark hair and a friendly, welcoming smile.

"I want to pick up a newspaper." Meghan smiled. You couldn't help but smile around Mr. Nak. His cheerful attitude just rubbed off. "I'm looking for a job, and I thought I might find something in the want ads."

Mr. Nak studied her for a second. "Aren't you working on the water taxi?"

"Yes," Meghan nodded, "but I need more hours."

Mr. Nak grinned. "Well, just maybe we can help each other out. I need a newspaper carrier for ten islands. Old Bart is moving to Florida, and I need to fill his position right away."

"Which islands?" Meghan asked curiously.

"The four Christmas Islands — Bethlehem, Jerusalem, Nazareth, and Galilee. Let's see," he scratched his head, "the Candy Islands — Gumdrop, M&M, Lollipop, and Hershey, and then No Name Island and Rose Island." Mr. Nak paused momentarily. "You know, they're all on the north side of the lake. You could probably deliver to all the islands within three hours. You deliver the newspaper to the mailbox houses on each island and then put them in the customer's box. If you get a system down, you could easily make all the deliveries before your water taxi schedule started."

"How much does it pay?"

"It pays $75.00 a week, but with tips, you could easily pull in $100. The customers are very grateful not to have to come to the mainland to get their daily papers."

Meghan nodded. "When do the papers have to be delivered by?"

Mr. Nak slowly smiled in such a way that Meghan knew she wasn't going to like the answer. "You'd have to be at the docks at Weir's Beach at 5:30."

"In the morning?" Meghan's voice came out sounding strained.

Mr. Nak laughed. "Yes, Meg. It's a morning paper. It wouldn't do me much good to have it delivered in the evening."

Meghan groaned. She was not a morning person. Getting up at seven was a major feat. Getting to Weir's Beach by 5:30 would be pure torture. She suddenly thought of the Taco man costume and inwardly cringed. She quickly decided that she could stand a certain torture over the daily humiliation that costume would bring. The early morning hours might kill her, but at least she'd die with her dignity intact. "OK," Meghan nodded at Mr. Nak, "I'll take the job. When do I start?"

"Tomorrow morning," Mr. Nak reached over and shook her hand. "Welcome aboard, Meghan Kane. It's going to be a pleasure doing business with you."

As Meghan exited the newspaper office, she did a few quick mental calculations. If she could pull in $100 a week, even if she had to give half of that to her dad for gas and wear and tear on the boat, she and Lindy could buy the food and clothes that they needed. It would be tight, and it would mean eating a lot of peanut butter and jelly sandwiches; but at least it would mean eating.

She smiled and sent a prayer heavenward thanking God for giving her a job. Lindy would love the early morning, and she would learn to tolerate it. The important thing was that their needs would be met. God was good. Once again He had rescued them, and she was grateful. Truly He was the father to the fatherless.

Seven

Meghan and Lindy, dressed in sweatshirts and jackets, started for Weir's Beach the next morning at 5:00 A.M. Meghan wanted to get to the docks a little early to familiarize herself with her new job.

Meghan glanced at her little sister. Lindy, who had always been a morning person, was thrilled at being told she could actually get up earlier. Meghan was not as enthusiastic about it; but every time she thought about the Taco man costume, she was incredibly grateful she didn't have to wear it. She needed this job to take care of Lindy and herself. As she watched her little sister at the front of the boat, her heart swelled with pride. She loved Lindy so much. All they had was each other and God in this great big world. For all the trouble and embarrassment that Lindy could give Meghan, when push came to shove, Lindy usually listened pretty well.

As Meghan continued to watch Lindy, she had to laugh. The little girl had gotten up early enough to find the time to put on her queen outfit. Lindy took the world on every morning decked out in full costume. Meghan smiled again. She liked the royal outfit. It suited Lindy well. She did have a touch of royal attitude.

As they passed Elizabeth Island, Lindy shouted excitedly. "Meghan! I see a big furry fish!"

Meghan looked in the direction that Lindy was now pointing in and smiled. "Lindy, that's not a big furry fish, that's a bear. It looks like he's swimming from Elizabeth Island to Victoria Island."

"I didn't know that bears could swim that far."

"They can swim miles if they have too," Meghan had heard many stories around the lake about swimming black bears. It was a weird experience to be half a mile from the nearest land and pass a bear in the middle of the lake.

"I like to watch him." The bear had Lindy's full attention. Meghan had to admit; it was interesting to watch the bear but not at all comforting. This would be a very bad time to break down. She didn't want to take the bear on as a passenger.

When they reached Weir's Beach, Mr. Nak met them at the dock. As he dropped the bundles of newspapers in Meghan's boat, Lindy chatted excitedly with him about the swimming bear.

"You need to be careful early in the morning. You're more likely to see all kinds of wild life."

Meghan laughed. "I don't mind seeing them, especially from a distance."

"You don't want to break down this early," Mr. Nak warned.

Meghan grinned. "I already figured that out."

After the paper bundles were loaded, Mr. Nak handed Meghan a bag of donuts and two cups of hot chocolate. "I thought you might appreciate this on your first morning."

"Thank you, Mr. Nak," Lindy excitedly took the bag of donuts. "Meghan and I would appreciate this anytime, not just this morning."

Meghan laughed. The little girl was a quick thinker. "Thanks a lot, Mr. Nak. This is going to be great."

As Meghan steered her boat toward the Christmas Islands, she told Lindy to sit down and eat. "A queen has to stand so she can wave to her people," Lindy informed Meghan firmly.

"There is no one else on the lake right now but us and a few black bears. Sit down, queen, and eat your breakfast."

Lindy turned her royal head and stared at Meghan. "No," she replied adamantly.

Meghan's eyes narrowed. Lindy was looking for a fight before six in the morning. She had enough trouble trying to think straight this early much less make Lindy behave. "If you don't sit down, I'm not giving you your hot chocolate. If you're standing, you'll spill it on yourself and get burned."

"I'm not sitting down." As if to prove the point, Lindy stuffed another piece of chocolate donut in her mouth and stared at her older sister defiantly.

Meghan shook her head. She knew sooner or later Lindy was going to need something to wash the donut down. When she did, she would come looking for her hot chocolate and Meghan would try again.

About five minutes later, Lindy walked to the back of the boat and stood in front of Meghan. The little girl had a painful expression on her face. Meghan wanted to laugh but she held it in. "Do you need a drink, Lindy?" The little girl nodded vigorously. "Are you going to sit down?"

Lindy stared at Meg for a minute and then reluctantly nodded. Meghan handed the cup of hot chocolate to her sister and watched her slowly make her way to the front of the boat. She stood at her post for a second, turned around to see if Meghan was watching her and then slowly sat down. Meghan smiled. Lindy was one tough cookie. She had no doubt the little girl could handle anything that life tossed her way.

The first island they approached was No Name. Meghan always thought that was a funny name for an island. It reminded her of the unique, Yankee sense of humor that was prevalent around the lake.

As they docked at No Name, Meghan and Lindy took the first bundle of newspapers and headed to the green and white mailbox house. The house was small, only about ten feet by twelve feet. It had three small windows that were trimmed out in white, on each side of the house and on the back of the house. A short flagpole on the top of the roof proudly displayed the red, white and blue American flag. The house looked more like a cute child's playhouse than it did a building designed to hold mailboxes. As the girls entered the house, there were shelves on every wall, stacked three layers high, with mailboxes on them. Meghan looked at the list of customers that Mr. Nak had given her and then she and Lindy started stuffing mailboxes.

Fifteen minutes later, they were off in the boat headed for the Christmas Islands. The Christmas Islands, Bethlehem, Jerusalem, Nazareth, and Galilee, were clumped fairly closed together. Just like Cedar Island and Pine Tree Island, docks had been built between the four islands for the kids to swim to. Meghan smiled. It looked like a lot of fun. One dock had a diving board and another one had a slide.

As Meg taxied her way in between Bethlehem and Jerusalem, the queen of the boat turned around. "Mary Beth Denton has chickens."

Meghan looked curiously at her little sister and wondered where the conversation was headed. You really never did know with Lindy. "You mentioned something about that yesterday." Meg grinned. "And, the day before and the day before that." When Lindy got an idea in her head she never gave up. "What's up Lindy?"

"Mary Beth has an egg route on Gumdrop Island."

Meghan studied her sister for a second. "OK," she shrugged, "you've got me. What's an egg route?"

Lindy lit up with excitement. Meghan didn't know how anyone could be that excited so early in the morning. It should be against the law. "An egg route is the same thing as a newspaper route but you deliver eggs instead of papers."

"That sounds like a good little business."

Lindy nodded and smiled. "Mary Beth has fifteen customers on Gumdrop Island and she makes twenty dollars a week."

"Really?" Meghan was surprised to think that any five-year-old kid could be making twenty bucks a week selling eggs.

"Yes," Lindy nodded seriously. She took a deep breath and then plunged into her spiel. "I want chickens, and I want an egg route. I was thinking that we could deliver the eggs the same time that we deliver the papers."

Meghan looked intently at the little determined girl in front of her before answering. "It's a good idea, Lindy, but raising chickens is a lot of work."

"I will take care of my chickens."

Meghan had to laugh. The chickens had already become her chickens. She was ready to roll. "You know that taking care of chickens doesn't just mean collecting their eggs. You'd have to clean up their poop too."

Lindy's enthusiasm dwindled momentarily. "Mary Beth explained all that to me. It's part of the business. She says you can use a shovel. You don't have to touch it with your hands."

Meghan paused thoughtfully. "When you buy chickens, it takes a while before they start laying eggs. It's not an immediate thing."

Lindy smiled proudly. "Mary Beth is moving in one week, and she still hasn't found anyone to take her chickens."

"Really?" Meghan didn't know why she should be surprised. Lindy was a businesswoman at heart and would have researched her proposal well.

Lindy nodded. "I want her chickens, and I want her egg route."

"I'll speak to dad about it, Lindy. If he says yes, we'll talk to the Denton's about taking the chickens."

"He will say yes," Lindy sounded confident. "He needs the money."

"Where did you hear that?"

"You know how I like to make a fort under Dad's old desk?" Meg nodded. "Well, he was on the phone

one day and I heard dad talking. He didn't know I was there."

"You shouldn't be listening to dad's phone conversations."

"I was there first," Lindy didn't see the need to apologize.

"You don't need to worry about money." Meghan assured her sister. "We're doing OK."

Lindy nodded, but her expression revealed that she didn't really believe what Meg was saying. "I still want the chickens."

"I'll talk to him today."

"I love you, Meghan," Lindy said straight from her heart.

Meghan felt overwhelmed by her emotions. "I love you, too, Squirt." Lindy had a way of sneaking over the wall that Meg had built around her heart. Lindy knew that Meg wasn't as tough as everyone thought she was and she was able to disarm her with just a simple word or a smile.

As the sisters went through the rest of the early morning hours, delivering the newspapers, Meghan's mind started thinking about other business opportunities that they could take advantage of. The islanders were always complaining about running out of the basic supplies. If she could start a business that provided them with the basic supplies, it might prove lucrative.

Meghan smiled. If she was going to the islands every day to deliver papers, delivering a few supplies would be no big deal. The only boat that brought food supplies to the islands was the U. S. Mail Boat. Meg smiled again. Daniel was the one in charge of the food supplies and the snack counter. Her smile grew wider. Maybe it was time to give Daniel Hatch a little competition. The more she thought about it the more she decided she would do it. She and Lindy would start a business delivering food supplies to the island. She wasn't going to put Daniel out of business but she did intend to give him a run for his money. It was the least she could do.

Eight

𝒯hree weeks had passed since Meghan had started her paper route. The day after the paper route started, her dad had said yes to the chicken idea. Mr. Denton put all thirty squawking chickens into cages and delivered them personally to Cedar Island. Web and Simon helped the girls build a chicken coop, and they found they were able to keep Mary Beth's customers very happy. Lindy was already dreaming of plans to expand but Meghan managed to keep that idea on hold for now.

The young entrepreneurs had left notices in their newspaper customer's mailboxes that if they wanted any groceries, the were to arrange a running tab with Kappies Grocery stores and then they would deliver the food for a service charge of five dollars.

The system worked better than the girls could imagine. They soon developed a regular group of grocery customers and delivered the sacks of food right to the mailbox house. Business was booming.

One morning as Meghan and Lindy ate their breakfast at Bug Lighthouse, a small powerboat came toward the island. The girls watched it curiously. As the boat docked, they both recognized the driver. "It's Daniel!" Lindy screamed excitedly. "I'm going to marry him some day."

"You can have him," Meghan felt anxious and angry at the same time.

Lindy ran off to greet Daniel, but Meghan stayed on the lighthouse keeper's porch and absent-mindedly fiddled with her granola bar. She tried to take the few minutes to prepare herself to see Daniel.

"How have you been?" Daniel studied her carefully. They had known each other too long and too well to play games with each other.

"Fine," Meg avoided his gaze as she tried to think of an excuse to leave.

An awkward silence grew between them. There was so much to say, Meghan thought as she played with her shoestring, and then again, really nothing to say at all. Daniel's actions over the past few weeks had said what his words had not. It was over. He had already moved on.

"So," he asked quietly as he sat down on the porch steps next to her, "are you trying to put me out of business?"

"What are you talking about?" Meg stole a sideways glance at him.

"Since you've been delivering snacks and groceries to the islands, my demand has gone way down."

Daniel's attempt to joke about the issue fell flat. "I never thought of you as my competition before."

"I'm not your competition, Daniel," Meghan couldn't conceal her irritation. "With all the snacks and food that the mail boat sells to all the other islands, the few that I service should be no big deal to you."

"Are you planning on expanding your route?"

Meghan narrowed her eyes at him. "That's really none of your business, is it?"

He stared at her for a second. "No," he admitted softly. "I was just curious."

"If we expand, it won't be very far." To service the other islands would take more time than she and Lindy had, but she didn't want to share that information with Daniel. She didn't want to share anything with him. Meghan found her emotions in an all out war between what she had with Daniel in the past and what she wouldn't have with him in the future. As much as she wanted to hate him, a part of her still loved him very much. She sighed. They had too much history together to end things so quickly. A part of her would probably always love Daniel and she hated that part of herself right now. The other part of her, which was rapidly gaining favor, wanted to cream him. She smiled. That part was going to win if she wasn't careful and right now she didn't feel like being very careful. Clobbering Daniel Hatch would probably be very therapeutic.

Meghan turned and looked at Daniel with clear annoyance. "Daniel, "she sighed, "what do you want?" Meg slid off the porch step that she was sitting on. "Lindy and I have to get to our route soon."

"I came for closure, Meg."

"I believe that already happened."

As he looked at her, Meghan could still see the love he felt for her in his eyes. It infuriated her to no end. Did he honestly think he could have things both ways? She would set that record straight immediately.

"Don't look at me that way, Daniel. You have no right to anymore. You made your choice, now live with it."

"Can you live with it?" His brown eyes searched hers tenderly. She wished she didn't find them so attractive. She was trying to be mad at him, not lose her heart to him every time she was around him.

"You know," Meghan answered strongly, "I didn't think I'd be able to. If you asked me that question a few months ago, I would have said definitely no."

"Now your answer has changed?"

"Yes, Daniel, you changed it for me. I was forced to see that I really can live without you. I think a more important question is can you really live without me?" Meghan watched him closely. "That's something that you're going to have to find out and then live with." She stared at him with all the fury that had been building up over the past weeks. "You will never get me back."

"Really?" His tone intended to challenge her, but it only angered her more. "We had something special for such a long time. Can you really give it up so easily?"

"Do you remember when I told you that I didn't have a choice about working? I had said that I felt so many choices in my life had been made for me and the only choice I had was how I would choose to accept them."

"I remember."

"Well, Daniel you took another choice away from me. Once again I found myself facing a decision in my life that I had nothing to do with. The only choice I had to make concerning our relationship was how I planned to get over you."

"That's not true."

Meghan sighed. "What part isn't true?" He dropped his eyes to avoid her penetrating look. "You know it's true," she whispered in a painful voice.

"One thing I have learned in life is that you don't always get the luxury of making a choice. Often times, the only choice I get is how I'm going to deal with a decision that has already been made for me." She looked him in the eyes. "That's what I had to do about the decision that you made about us."

"So, you just made a decision to get over me?"

"Yes, I did."

Daniel ran a hand through his short brown hair. "Ya know, I didn't plan to start liking Brittany."

Meghan suddenly realized that she was holding her breath. He actually admitted it right to her face. She was shocked by his honesty, and yet strangely relieved at the same time. Somehow, Meghan finally found her voice. "I didn't think she was your type, Daniel."

"She's not what you think, Meg." He was actually defending her. Meg smiled knowingly. He had to defend Brittany because by defending Brittany he was really defending himself and the decision that he had made. "She's not what you think. Once you get to know her, she's very nice."

Meghan ground her teeth together for a moment to keep from saying something that she knew she would one day, far in the future regret. She took a deep breath and then tried to speak calmly. "People who are really nice don't treat other people like dirt."

"She's misunderstood."

Meghan sighed at his weak defense. If he were a lawyer he would lose this case for sure. "Daniel, I'm going to be honest with you because I've always been honest with you. I think you are the only person on the lake that thinks that Brittany Bentley is misunderstood. I think you misunderstand her. She has earned herself quite a reputation. She's been nasty to so many people I can't understand how you can be so blind to it." Meghan took another deep breath. "She's not a nice person, Daniel. You don't see her for how she really is."

"And why wouldn't I?" he demanded angrily.

Meghan glanced at him and felt a small amount of sympathy. Honesty hurt at times and this time it was digging in painfully deep. "You're caught up with a rich, popular, pretty girl who wears clothes too tight and has very big…hair." Daniel's eyes narrowed and Meghan simply laughed. "You must think I'm blind not to notice. Come on…"

"You are so far wrong."

"Daniel, even if everything I just said wasn't true, which it is, there's something that is completely true. Brittany is not even a Christian. That used to be important to you at one time."

Daniel was steaming. She could see the heat in his eyes. "For your information, Brittany became a Christian at the Michael W. Smith concert."

Meghan's mouth dropped open in pure shock. For several moments, she was too stunned to speak. Daniel had just sunk to a new low level that she didn't think he was capable of sinking to. "Let me get this straight," Meg put a hand up in the air, "are you telling me that you brought Brittany Bentley to the concert with my ticket?" Meghan searched his eyes for the truth. "Daniel, tell me that's not true."

"I had to go with somebody," he admitted quietly.

Meghan felt like she had just been kicked in the stomach. Now the truth was hurting her. "I can't believe you. We were still engaged at that time." Meghan wiped her unexpected tears away. "Daniel, how could you?"

He couldn't look her in the eye. "You couldn't go and I had an extra ticket. She did become a Christian Meg. You should be glad. She's different."

"You went with her to get me back for not going, didn't you?" He didn't answer and Meghan turned and began to walk down the narrow dirt path that led to her boat.

As she glanced over her shoulder, she was more annoyed than surprised to see that Daniel had followed her. She stopped and turned to face him. "You knew I didn't have a choice about working. How can you be mad at me for that?"

"You were working so much that I never saw you anymore."

"Why didn't you ride along on the taxi like Web and Simon did? We could have spent more time together than we ever had."

"Things didn't work out that way." He sighed loudly as he scuffed his sneaker in the dirt. "Brit's really different."

Meghan sighed loudly. "So am I." Meg turned and continued walking back to her boat. "I'm not the same trusting idiot that I was a month ago." She cast a hard look at Daniel. " I have you to thank for that."

"Meghan," Daniel pleaded, "we need to talk this through." He reached out and took her hand to hold her back. "I still want us to be friends."

"Don't you dare touch me," Meghan pulled her hand from his. "Don't you ever touch me again. You have no right."

"I want for us to be friends," Daniel's voice was earnest.

"Are you even kidding? That's not going to happen. Get real. Did you honestly think that you could have both Brittany and me? What were you hoping to do, Daniel? Were you going to date her while you string me along?" Meghan felt her fists ball in anger. "When we got engaged, you asked me to wait for you." Meghan yanked the sapphire engagement ring out of her pocket and shoved it into Daniel's hand. "I won't wait for you anymore, Daniel. I'll never wait for you again."

Nine

Meghan tried hard to push the events with Daniel out of her mind. Today was a day that she had looked forward to for a long time. She didn't want anything ruining it for her and that included Daniel Hatch. She wanted him to be a distant memory, but she honestly knew he wasn't going to fade out quickly enough for her.

She and Lindy were heading towards Weir's Beach to pick up Roy and Ray Hobson. They were Miss Grace's brothers, and they came to visit her every summer during the month of August. For the rest of the year, the two elderly brothers lived at the Sugar Creek Inn in Maine.

Meghan smiled at the thought of the Hobson's. The two brothers were such a comical pair. They were funny, charming as could be and kind to a fault. Every August, Meghan and Lindy both felt like they had two wonderful, dotting grandfathers. It was almost too good to be true.

As Meghan's boat approached Weir's Beach, she could see Roy and Ray waiting for her on the dock. Their luggage was next to them and they both waved as soon as they spotted her. Meghan laughed. Simon and Webster were with them too and the four of them looked like they were having a party.

As she pulled the boat up next to the dock, Web grabbed the boat lines and anchored her. "Hey," Web's eyes glowed excitedly, "look who we found hanging around the dock."

Meghan smiled. The Hobson brothers had been coming to Lake Winnipesaukee since before she was born. They were always a highlight of her summer, and she loved the two elderly brothers with all her heart. Too bad they weren't sixty years younger, Meg mused. They'd be perfect.

"It's good to see you, young lady," Roy wrapped his arms around her. "Always a pleasure, my dear."

"Good to see you, too, Roy," Meghan suddenly felt very emotional.

The old country doctor eyed her sternly. "You look tired, Meghan."

Meg laughed. "You say that every time you see me."

Roy nodded. "That may be so, but this time I mean it. You look very tired."

"She works all the time," Web volunteered. "The only way Simon and I get to see her is if we ride along with her as she does her taxi routes."

Roy's eyebrows shot up. "Is that true?"

"Web exaggerates," Meghan shrugged off his concern, but she knew that Roy wasn't buying it.

"Stop hogging the prettiest girl on the lake." Ray pushed his way forward and hugged Meghan. "I have missed you, dear." Ray held Meghan at arms length for a moment. "I hate to admit this, but Roy is right. You do look tired."

"I'm fine." Meghan knew it was time to change the subject. "Hey, tell me what's new at Sugar Creek Inn?"

The two brothers looked at her and laughed. "You can't fool us, my dear." Roy chuckled again. "Nice try, but I just want you to know that your diversion tactic failed."

Meghan grinned. They were too sharp for their own good. She didn't need someone telling her that she was tired. She already knew that. "Time to head off for Evergreen Island. We don't want to keep Miss Grace waiting."

"Maybe you don't," Ray laughed, "but I really don't mind. I think I've kept her waiting most of my life. If I start to be on time at my age, she's going to come to expect it." He slanted a grin at Meg. "That could be trouble."

Lindy came over and wiggled herself between the two brothers. "And who are you, young lady?" Roy asked curiously.

"She's looks a little bit like a girl we once knew named Lindy but you can't be her because you're so grown up looking."

Lindy beamed proudly. "I am Lindy!"

The brothers acted completely shocked. "No…" Roy turned and looked at the little girl closely. "You can't be the Lindy I was talking about. I was talking about Lindy Kane."

"I am Lindy Kane."

"You mean that you are the Lindy Kane that's Meghan Kane's sister?" Ray asked adjusting his glasses.

"Yes, I am." Lindy was becoming impatient.

"Hey Meghan," Roy tried to conceal his smile, "this isn't your little sister Lindy Kane, is it?"

Meghan laughed. Lindy looked like she was no longer enjoying the fact that they didn't recognize her. Lindy was one girl who loved self-recognition. "That's her," Meghan admitted quickly. "You probably didn't recognize her because she grew up so much since last summer."

"Wow," Ray put an arm around the little girl, "it is you."

"I told you so," Lindy sounded more disgusted than pleased.

"You're so grown up," Roy started buttering her up. Lindy began to smile again.

"Just yesterday, a lady asked me if I was seven," Lindy shared this news with great pride. "When I told her I was only five, she said she couldn't believe it."

"I can see how that would happen," Ray winked at her.

"Do you like my crown?" Lindy adjusted the gold crown.

"Very much," Roy smiled. "That's probably why I didn't recognize you. The crown makes you look so much older."

"I am the Queen of England," Lindy stood up and showed them her royal pose.

"I would say you make a very fine queen, Lindy. Here," Ray stuck out his hand, "shake my hand. I've never had the honor of shaking a queen's hand before."

Lindy solemnly shook his hand and then turned around to shake Roy's hand. Both men's eyes were lit with twinkles. "You look lovely," Roy whispered.

"So, tell me queen," Ray asked interestedly, "what has gone on in your life during this past year besides you becoming a member of the royal family?"

Lindy excitedly began chattering non-stop about the newspaper route, the egg route, and the water taxi. She ended the summary of her life by saying that Daniel Hatch had dumped Meghan and was now dating a girl that used to be naked.

In unison, Roy and Ray Hobson both turned and looked at Meghan with questioning eyes. They were patiently waiting for her explanation to this interesting story. Meghan could only imagine what they thought about Daniel dating a naked girl. That would be a story all in itself.

As Meghan was carefully formulating a very generic sounding answer in her mind, a new black jet ski pulled up along side of the water taxi. "Hey, Meghan, do you want to race?"

Meghan didn't know if she were more shock that Reid Kensington had pulled up along side of her boat, or that he looked so excited to see her. She wondered what the Perfect Prince wanted. They didn't exactly run in the same circles. Reid ran with the fast, the popular, and the extremely good-looking "A" crowd group. Meghan puttered around somewhere in the B group and was quite happy to be there.

"Not today, Reid," Meghan answered the handsome teenager. She bit her lip to keep from smiling. Reid Kensington really was one of God's masterpieces. He had blonde hair, deep blue eyes that seem to glow from his excitement, a charm that none could master and a self confidence that wasn't exactly cocky but as close to it as you could come without crossing over the line. The man looked perfect, even when he was on a jet ski soaking wet.

Meghan thought Reid was going to zoom away, but he surprised her again and continued the conversation as though he were in no hurry to go anywhere. "Hey, I was wondering if you were going to the big party at Weir's Beach on Saturday night?"

"Go away, Reid," Simon ordered his older brother in a less than friendly way.

Reid completely ignored him and looked back at Meghan. "You see," he flashed a wonderfully white, perfect-looking smile at her, "if you were going then I was wondering if you would do me the great honor of going with me?" Meghan was so startled by the invitation that she almost steered her boat into Reid's jet ski. Reid pulled away to avoid a collision and then veered back towards her. "I can pick you up at seven."

Somehow Meghan found her voice. "I didn't say yes."

Reid grinned at her captivatingly. "Yes, I know that, but I also noticed that you didn't say no either. I'm hoping that means you're considering it. I think we'd have a great time together."

Meghan cast a quick glance at the Hobson brothers. They looked as shocked as she was, and they weren't even trying to hide their surprise. Their mouths hung open slightly, and they stared at Meghan waiting for her to make the next move.

Meghan couldn't seem to make her mind work. Never in all the years that she had lived on the lake had Reid showed so much interest in her. "Uh, I think that I may be working that night."

"Is that a no?" Reid leaned a bit closer to her.

"That's how a polite girl tells you no, Reid." Simon looked more than disgusted. "Go away."

"Listen," Reid continued casually, "I'm not going to bring a date. If you show up, I'll give you a ride home if you'd like. No pressure. We'll just hang out." Before Meg could answer, Reid sped off on his jet ski flying across the water faster than her taxi could ever dream of going.

"Well…" Roy drew the single word out longer than a full sentence could be spoken, "I can definitely see that we've missed a lot this past year."

"Not really," Meghan mumbled.

The Hobson's chuckled. "I hate to disagree with you so soon in the vacation Meg, but I know what I saw." Ray winked at her.

Meghan stared at the elderly man. "What is it that you think you saw Ray?"

Ray's eyes twinkled, and he smiled knowingly. "I may be old, dear, but I'm not blind. The Perfect Prince just asked you out on a date."

Roy laughed. "You know, news like this is just going to infuriate the Hatch boy and his naked friend." The men shared another laugh together.

"I don't think Daniel's going to find out about his," Meghan kept her voice as non-interested as she could.

Ray laughed. "Are you kidding? He'll find out. This is front-page news."

Meghan silenced him with a look. "There is no news, Ray. There's nothing to tell."

"Now don't go getting all huffy with me but I think that everyone on this boat would probably disagree with you. This is news and there's a lot to tell."

"I didn't say that I'd go with him."

Ray grinned. "Now you see, the interesting thing about that answer you gave him, not that I was eavesdropping or anything…"

"Oh, of course not, not you two," Meghan said sarcastically.

"I was simply here. I couldn't help but listen," Ray tried to justify himself, "anyways, what I'm trying to say is that you didn't turn the scoundrel down. You left the door open, and that is the thing that gossip is made of. The possibility that you will go with him is there."

"I wasn't planning on going anywhere with Reid." Meghan hoped this would end the discussion, but she soon found that to be wrong.

"He's a scoundrel," Roy agreed. "Stay away from him. Leave things to Ray and I. We'll find you a nice boy."

"No!" Meghan shouted. "You will not."

Roy looked puzzled. "You don't think I can find you a nice boy?"

"I don't want to enlist your match making services."

"I do know a lot of nice boys. If you tell me what you're looking for, I'll check my files."

"I mean it, Roy. Stay out of it." She couldn't believe she was having this conversation with them.

"Are you planning on picking us up for the card game later in the week?" Ray asked.

Meghan stared at him. "Only if you promise to be good."

"That's a yes," Roy smiled and ignored her hard look. "You see, that will give us plenty of time to talk you out of dating the scoundrel."

"I'm not dating Reid." Meghan was becoming angry.

"That's right you're not. Ray and I won't allow it."

The conversation finally ended but no one seemed to notice how quiet Simon had become. Behind his sunglasses, his eyes were shooting out volcanic sparks. He would be having a talk with his brother well before Saturday night's beach party; and for once in his life, he didn't feel the slightest bit intimidated by the great Reid Kensington.

Ten

"Stay away from Meghan Kane." Simon glared at his brother angrily.

Reid's face showed the astonishment that he felt inside. It was a rare occasion that his quiet, younger brother raised his voice to him. The surprise quickly left Reid as curiosity filled its place.

"Why, Simon?" Reid lowered his black designer sunglasses just slightly to get a better look at him. "Why is it so important to you that I stay away from Meghan? You've never cared about the other girls that I pursued."

The brothers were in lounge chairs by the lake at their family estate. At a casual glance, they looked relaxed and seemed to be enjoying themselves; but they were anything but relaxed and definitely not enjoying themselves.

"Just stay away from Meghan," Simon ordered.

A slow smile crossed Reid's face. "I'd like a reason."

"I can give you a thousand."

Reid laughed. "Just one or two will do."

"She's not your type." Simon looked directly at his brother. Reid was so confident and smug at the moment that he actually felt like punching him.

"Care to expand on that?" he asked with an annoying calmness to his voice.

"She doesn't fool around, Reid. She's a nice girl." Simon took off his sunglasses and fiddled with them. "Even when she was engaged to Daniel Hatch, she didn't fool around."

Reid smiled wickedly. "Now you see," he slapped his brother on the back, "that's just the type of girl that I'm looking for." He stood up and began to pace. "I'm changing my ways Simon. I no longer want to be known as the perfect little prince." He ran a hand through his short blonde hair. "If I'm going to run for office in a few years I need to start polishing my image now. I need to start planning and preparing for it." He laughed. "It takes time to perfect the squeaky clean all American boy image that people love so much."

"Just how exactly does Meghan fit into your plans?" Simon darted an irritated look at him.

"She's just the type of girl I need Simon. Meghan will help complete the wholesome image that I'm trying to portray."

"Do you even like her, or is this purely for political reasons?"

Reid gazed thoughtfully at Simon for a moment before answering. "Back down, Simon. I'm not going to hurt her." He sighed loudly. "I know I've been a real jerk at times in the past, but I'm honestly trying to change my ways. I don't think I can stand another day of the empty life I was living. It took me this long to figure out that there was no point to it. I had the girls, the money, the fame," Reid sighed, "and all it left me so completely empty inside, I wanted to die. I need to change, Simon," his voice had taken on an urgency that Simon rarely heard from his brother. "I'm only eighteen, and I've already figured out that my life is not worth living the way it is. The way I'm going, I'm going to crash and burn for sure. There's no point to anything in my life. There's got to be more, ya know?"

Simon knew his brother well enough to know that his intentions were honest. The struggle inside him was evident in the pained expression on his face. Could his brother really be looking for truth and God after all these years? Simon felt overwhelmed by Reid's disclosure. "I understand your struggle," Simon said compassionately. "I have been telling you for years that God is the only thing in this life worth living for."

"Well, maybe I'm just starting to understand that."

"What does all this have to do with Meghan? There are plenty of other girls you could pursue."

Reid shook his head. "A part of me has always loved and admired Meghan. She's different than any of the other girls I've known." Reid grinned. "And I've known a lot of girls…."

Simon laughed. "You'll get no argument from me on that subject."

"I'm really ashamed of how I've handled myself in the past. I want to start over with a clean slate."

Simon couldn't believe what he was hearing. "Are you serious?"

"Totally," Reid nodded. "Meghan is the girl for me. She isn't afraid to take a stand even when she's standing alone." Reid sighed. "I admire how she's raised Lindy and taken on so many jobs to keep her and Lindy and the marina afloat. Most kids wouldn't do that. Meg is a survivor. She's very special."

"She'd never become one of your adoring fans." Simon's voice was factual. "Meghan wouldn't drop at your feet like all the other girls do."

Reid laughed. "I admire her for that, too. Meghan wouldn't be afraid to speak her mind to me. When I head to Washington, DC, that's exactly the type of wife I need. She'll be quite an asset to my campaign as well. Meghan speaks easily with others, and people are naturally drawn to her. She's a person that speaks from her heart. That's a rare quality in today's world."

Simon shook his head as Reid dropped back into his lounge chair again. "I see a few problems with your plan."

Reid grinned. "I'm good at fixing problems."

"First off, Meghan would never date you because you're not a Christian. Her faith is very important to her. It's the thing that has kept her going in all those tough times." Simon paused. "As hard as it may be for you to believe, Meghan wouldn't ever ditch God for you. He's too important in her life."

Reid grinned again. "You see, that's another reason I like Meghan, and that's also a part of my plan."

"I'm not following you."

"I feel a good Senator should have a firm religious background. I'm planning on attending church and gaining a solid background of what Meghan believes. If it's worked so well for the two of you, I think I should take the time to check it out for myself."

"I think you should check out God, but you should do it with an honest seeking heart not as another peg in your political portfolio. If your intentions aren't aboveboard, Meghan will see right through you. She can spot a fake a hundred miles away."

"She won't see right through me if I'm sincere."

"Are you planning on being sincere?" Simon almost couldn't believe it.

"Yes I am, Simon. My past is not a thing that I'm particularly proud of. I'm trying to change that. All

I ask is that you give me the benefit of the doubt. Give me a change to prove I'm changing."

"I'll try." He felt sick inside thinking of his brother going after sweet, innocent Meghan. She was too good for him. "You know that she's still in love with Daniel. I don't think she'd date anyone right now, including someone as charming and handsome as you."

"We'll see." Reid laughed. "Good old Daniel Hatch. He really made my job so much easier by breaking up with Meghan. I wasn't sure what I was going to do after he gave her that engagement ring." Reid laughed again. "That's the only reason that I'm thankful that Brittany is on the lake. You know," Reid turned and looked at his brother thoughtfully, "I'm honestly surprised that a good Christian boy like Daniel Hatch would be reeled in by a brat like Brittany." He paused. "She's good looking enough, but she's so conceited and self absorbed. She's a very unpleasant person to be around."

"She hasn't change since childhood." Simon played with his sunglasses again. "She was always so full of herself."

"Does Daniel know that we have gone to prep school with Brit for most of our lives? Someone should explain to him that he's dating a girl whose past is more colorful than mine."

"I tried to talk to him, but he won't listen."

"He was blinded by her looks. If he doesn't be careful, he's going to become just another one of her casualties."

"I know," Simon agreed.

"I bet most people on the lake assumed I would go after Brittany."

"I think many were surprised that you didn't," Simon agreed. "But they don't know her like we do. I'm glad you stayed away from her, Reid."

"Simon, I never gave her a second thought." Reid shook his head. "I'm really disappointed in Daniel that he got suckered in by her."

"So am I." Simon gazed out across the lake. "You know, Meg's loved Hatch for most of her life. Do you honestly think that she's going to fall for your charming ways overnight?"

Reid smiled. "With a little help from me, Daniel Hatch will be nothing more than a distant memory for Meg."

"So," Simon cast an angry look at Reid, "you're planning on pursing Meghan as a challenge; and once you get her to fall in love with you dump, her like all the others."

Reid laughed. "Simon, you haven't been listening very well to what I've been saying. I'm planning on pursuing Meghan, and once she falls in love with me, I'm planning on asking her to marry me."

Simon turned and stared at Reid in disbelieve. "You've never mentioned the M word in your life."

"I want to marry Meghan. I've given this a lot of thought." Reid paused. "I'm very serious about this.

"She'll never marry you."

"I'll keep after her until she does." Reid stood up again and began to pace. "I'm a man who knows what he wants, and what I want more than anything in this world is Meghan Kane. I've wanted her a long time, but just now I'm getting the courage to go after her."

"You've got to be kidding? You never mentioned her before." Reid laughed. "Because you'd never believe that I liked her. You always thought I went after society girls."

"That's because you did."

"That's because I wasn't ready to go after Meghan. She was too young. Now that she's sixteen going on seventeen, I'd say it's time to let her know how I feel." Reid exhaled loudly. "I'll win her, Simon. Mark my words, I'll win Meghan as my wife."

Simon looked away and tried to swallow the growing lump in his throat. Reid had never lost a race or competition in his life. Whenever he went after something, he went after it with all his heart. He was persistent like no one else Simon knew and had enough patience to hang in there until things went his way. He never saw failure as an option. He simply hung in there and changed his plans until they happened for him.

He silently prayed that this would be the first competition that the great Reid Kensington lost. Meghan deserved so much better than Reid. He prayed that she would be able to resist his charming ways and not be swept off her feet by him. If she did, Simon knew that she would be the first girl to do so. When it came to romance, Reid was in a class all his own. He was extremely good-looking and very polished and debonair. He had always gotten the girl he went after.

Simon prayed that Reid wouldn't get Meghan. He didn't want to have to pick up the pieces of her heart as his suave, smooth operating brother broke it. He would. Simon knew he would. Reid had always broken girls' hearts and now he knew that his sophisticated, regal brother was about to ruin Meghan's life. Simon sighed. He was going to have to watch it all play out, and he knew there wasn't going to be a thing he could do to stop it.

Eleven

Meghan instinctively braced herself. She was delivering a group of seniors to their weekly bridge game on Evergreen Island. Meghan gripped the wheel firmly. Going to Evergreen Island meant that they had to pass through Pirates Cove and alarmingly close to the Baker boy's tree fort. Going close to the tree fort always had negative consequences.

Travis, Tommy and Timmy Baker were identical triplets and commonly referred to around the lake as the Triple Trouble. They were well-established juvenile delinquents on their way to committing some serious crimes.

Their father, Trent Baker, was a self-made billionaire. He owned several large construction companies and was responsible for many of the larger malls that went up throughout New England. Due to his overwhelmingly busy schedule, Trent was oftentimes not around to spend time with his boys much less have any kind of a hand in disciplining them. Using their father's finances and their never-ending creative imaginations, the boys terrorized anyone who dared to enter Pirates Cove.

When you passed by the Baker property, the first thing you noticed was their vast estate. Many of the tourists thought it was an island resort. The main house was a rambling white colonial mansion that was neatly tucked between pine trees and evergreen trees. The property line extended the entire south side of Evergreen Island. The land was decorated with tennis courts, a swimming pool, a full basketball court and a waterfront that was more impressive than any other on the lake. The Baker's had six sailboats, two catamarans, six jet skis, two wind surfers and a fleet of powerboats that looked like they belonged in the U.S. Coast Guard.

The thing that most people didn't see at first, but never forgot once they'd been under attack by it was the Baker boy's tree fort. Trent Baker had spent sixty thousand dollars building his eleven-year-old boys the most elaborate tree fort that Meghan had ever seen. It really wasn't a tree fort at all; it was more like a small house that had been built up in the trees.

The fort was dark stained pine with green trim. It looked like a storybook house with all the sharp peaks and steep angles that the roofline took. The fort was three levels; one for each son, and each level had a wrap around balcony.

Ropes, cables and an elaborate pulley line system had been set up so the boys could transport anything, including themselves to different parts of the fort.

They could go down one side of the house and then jump onto a zip line that was hidden beneath the floor. To get back up into the fort they could take the stairs or use a rock system that had been installed and climb the side of the fort like rock climbers would do. For quick emergency escapes, there was a slide that would shoot the boys right into Lake Winnipesaukee. It was an unbelievable place that both kids and grown-ups alike envied.

It seemed far too appropriate that these little tyrants would live on Pirates Cove. They were like pirates, taking great joy in attacking anyone who entered the cove. Meghan glanced at the tree fort again. The boys had taken a dream fort and turned it into a battleground for boaters. Meghan eyed the cannon on the top deck wearily.

The Triple Trouble would load the cannon with anything from water balloons to rotten tomatoes. Then they'd fire on the unsuspecting boaters as they passed the fort. Their success rate was alarmingly accurate. More than one person on the lake was screaming for revenge.

Suddenly Meghan spotted the boys. They were on the top floor of the tree fort playing with their giant slingshot. The boys loaded the slingshot full of the same ammo that they used in the cannon. This gave them two chances to hit their victims and usually both shots hit their targets.

"If they shoot that thing off," Web eyed the boys suspiciously, "I'm going to collect whatever garbage they throw at me and dump it over them." Web looked at Meghan. "Those little brats target me all the time. I've had it. Next time I get hit, it's going to mean war!"

"I'm with you, Web." Simon never took his eyes off the fort. "I feel like any time I enter Pirates Cove, I'm taking a huge risk of being plastered with garbage."

A slow grin swept across Simon's face. "Last week," he laughed, "the little creeps bombed Reid when he was on his jet ski. He came home covered with tomatoes stains on his new Ralph Lauren polo shirt." Simon laughed loudly. "I laughed so hard I almost wet my pants."

Meghan laughed. "I bet the Perfect Prince didn't take that well."

Simon shook his head. "No, he didn't. If you're going to plan a war Web, I'm sure Reid's going to want in on it. He's still pretty mad."

Meghan laughed. "And you still think it's pretty funny."

Simon laughed again. "Hey, it's not every day I get to see the great Reid Kensington covered in tomatoes stains. It's something that will make me smile for years to come."

"I'll bet," Web joined in their laughter. "Hitting Reid takes a lot of guts."

"Or stupidity," Simon acknowledged. "Reid doesn't take anything from anyone. Mark my words...my brother will seek revenge by the end of the summer."

"He won't be alone," Web mumbled.

"Seriously," Simon looked at Web, "If you want to start a war with the Baker brats, count Reid and I in."

Meghan laughed. "Anyone who lives on this side of the lake and has had to pass through Pirates Cove would help you."

"Would you join our war?" Web looked at Meghan questioningly.

Meghan nodded. "Both Lindy and I would. The Baker boys bombed us last week with eggs and ruined Lindy's royal dress. She's still really mad."

"Did she cry?" Simon asked in a concerned voice.

Meghan laughed. "Not Lindy. She was screaming for revenge and waving her royal scepter at them." Meg smiled. "I think if her scepter was a magic wand she would have turned them into toads or something. She's ready for battle."

Meghan breathed a sigh of relief as they made it through the cove. She smirked. It was a rare day that you made it through without getting fired upon.

Meghan eyed her elderly passengers with concern. They always became quite tense as they made it through the cove. The invasion by the boys had become so bad that Meghan always traveled through the cove with two or three garbage can lids to use as shields against the flying debris. She glanced at Web and Simon. They both had a lid, ready to use if necessary.

"Someone has got to teach those boys a lesson," Ray Hobson shook his head disapprovingly. "I hate having to pass by Pirate's Cove to get to Gracie's house." He darted a look at Web. "Those boys have got to be stopped."

"Why hasn't anyone spoken to the authorities about the little varmints?" Roy asked.

Meghan glanced at the elderly brothers compassionately. They were too old to endure pranks like this. "We think Mr. Baker has paid someone off."

"Sheriff Jimmy Stewart would never take a bride," Roy stated adamantly.

"No," Meg agreed, "it's not him. Mr. Baker has gone over his head. Jimmy says there's nothing that he can do about it, and I know it really steams him. He doesn't like to feel helpless."

Web laughed. "Sheriff Stewart is definitely not helpless when it comes to handing out speeding tickets."

"What did he nail you for?" Simon asked curiously.

"I had to pay him a hundred dollars."

"For what?" Meg gasped.

"For speeding on my scooter! Can you believe it?"

"How fast were you going?" Meghan narrowed her eyes. She knew Webster T. Long well enough to know that he wasn't entirely innocent.

"That's really not important," Web brushed aside her question.

Simon and Meghan laughed. "Come on," Simon grinned, "how fast were you going?"

"Forty-five."

"You were going forty-five miles per hour on a scooter!" Simon's eyes bugged out. "Scooter's top out at thirty."

Web grinned proudly. "Not mine."

"And the reason for that is?" Meg asked.

"Let's just say that I made a few minor adjustments."

"Where did you get pulled over?" Simon couldn't help but smile at his friend.

"In front of Kennedy Elementary School."

"Were the kids around the school?" Simon asked.

"They were loading up on their little yellow buses."

Meghan shook her head. "You were speeding in a school zone when the kids were getting out of school?"

Web shrugged. "It's not like I was going to hit any of them. Honestly Meg. Don't act like my father."

"You deserved your ticket, man," Simon patted him on the back. "And if I were your parent, I'd have taken away your scooter. You're going to get yourself killed on that thing."

As Meghan dropped the seniors off at Miss Gracie's to play cards, Roy shot a look of concern at Meghan. "Is there anyway to get out of this cove besides passing in front of suicide fort?"

Meghan shook her head grimly. "I wish there was, Roy. This is the only passageway that's deep enough to accommodate the boat. The other side of Evergreen Island is too rocky and too shallow."

"I feel like I'm doomed," Roy muttered.

Meghan laughed. "You're not the only one."

"If I were you, I'd declare an all out war on those scoundrels. This should not be just a defensive game; it should be an offensive game as well. It's time to make those boys pay."

"If we get hit one more time, there will be a war, Ray!" Web waved the garbage can lid in the air like a shield.

"Can we help plan the attack?" Ray asked excitedly. "Roy and I are very good at this sort of thing. We have been in the undercover business for years now. I really think we can be quite useful."

Meghan smirked at the two brothers. She had heard plenty about their undercover work from Miss Gracie, their sister. Roy and Ray were known to hide in hall closets and large bushes just to spy on people. Meghan laughed. They were worse than kids.

"Sure you can help us plan." Web smiled. "When we attack them, I'm planning on winning the war. It has to be successful enough so that they won't want to bomb anyone ever again."

"I'm sure we can help." Roy's eyes twinkled excitedly. "Call us when it's time."

As the water taxi made it's way back through Pirate's Cove, Meghan, Web, Simon and Lindy were the only ones aboard. The Baker boys had waited patiently for them knowing what comes into the cove has got to come out. They bombed Meg's boat with a variety of rotten vegetables, eggs, and water balloons. With the three boys launching their ammo from various directions, it was inevitable that they were going to get creamed.

As fate would have it, Web seemed to take the brunt of the attack. His Afro had tomatoes seeds stuck in it and two eggs had made direct contact with his shirt. Web stood up in the boat and waved his garbage can lid at the boys. "This is war! Do you hear me! This is war!"

Twelve

$\mathcal{B}$y the time that Meghan and Lindy had arrived at Weir's Beach for the summer beach party, things were well underway. The boardwalk was jam packed full of people, the docks were filled with boats, and the amusement park had all kinds of ride going, zinging people in all kinds of unnatural, sickening motions.

Meghan glanced over at the beach. Volleyball nets had been set up and a major volleyball tournament was underway. ESPN and NESN were covering the tournament for TV.

"I want to be on TV." Lindy immediately changed directions and began walking toward the tournament.

"Lindy, only the players are on TV."

"Then I want to play." She turned and looked up at her sister determinedly. "I want to be on TV. All my friends will see me and think I'm a movie star."

Meghan smiled. She knew it wouldn't help to point out that all her friends were probably at the beach party and not home watching TV. "You need to be in a movie to be a movie star."

Lindy stared at her. "Everyone needs to start somewhere. Let's go. I want to be on TV."

Meghan tried to reason with a very unreasonable Lindy. "Honey, these are professional volleyball players from all over the country. Meghan paused and watched a guy jump above the volleyball net and spike the ball practically down the opposing player's throat. "You see the way he hit that ball?" Lindy nodded. "Do you think you could do that?"

"I don't think I want to do that." Lindy frowned. Her dreams of stardom were beginning to take a more realistic turn.

Meghan ran a hand through Lindy's long brown hair. "Neither could I, Squirt. What do you say we go and get some food?" Lindy nodded but was still watching the volleyball game. Meg laughed. She knew that Lindy was still trying to figure out a way to get on TV.

Mr. Ward was running the hot dog stand, and Meghan went up to him and order two hot dogs and two orange sodas. Once they got their food, they made their way to an empty bench on the boardwalk.

Just as they sat down, Brittany Bentley rounded the corner. She stared at Meghan and Lindy a second before approaching them. Lindy spotted Brittany coming towards them right away. Even though her mouth was filled with hot dog, she managed to garble out an announcement. "Look, Meg, here comes the naked girl."

"Quiet, Lindy," Meghan ordered. Brittany Bentley had made a life long impression on Lindy as the naked girl. It didn't matter if she was wearing a ski suit or a bathing suit, Lindy would forever refer to her as the naked girl.

Brittany Bentley, aka, the naked girl, had already heard Lindy. She was staring at the little girl with an angry expression across her glamorized face. She wore more different kinds of makeup than Meghan even knew existed.

Meghan didn't like the look or the way that Brittany was coming toward them. She put her hot dog down on the bench and stood up to face the Malibu Barbie doll that was fast approaching.

"What did she call me?" Brittany demanded as she impatiently played with the straw in her Diet Coke.

"She called you the naked girl," Meghan answered flatly. She felt no threat from Brittany, only annoyance.

Brittany took a step closer to her as Daniel, Web, Simon and Reid rounded the corner. "And why would she call me that?" She rolled her eyes dramatically at Meg.

Lindy, who had decided that she wanted a piece of the action came up and stood bravely next to her sister. "I called you the naked girl," Lindy announced loudly, "because the first time I saw you, you weren't wearing any clothes."

"I was wearing a bathing suit." Brittany had gone from annoyed to indignant. It was too much for her that a five year old would not only stand up to her, but embarrass her as well.

"It was a really, really, tiny bathing suit." Lindy took another bite of her hot dog. "Everyone thought you were naked," Lindy mumbled with her mouth full.

As Brittany took a step toward Lindy, Meghan stepped in front of her and crossed her arms defensively. It was a clear warning not to approach her sister. Brittany turned her striking blue, fiery eyes on Meghan. She smiled coyly and played with her straw again. Meghan knew that verbal warfare was about to begin.

"I believe I have something of yours." She swung her eyes toward Daniel. "Does it still hurt?" She appeared innocent as a child and lethal as a serpent all at the same time. Meghan didn't know how she managed to pull it off.

"Brittany, don't!" Daniel had stepped up next to her. "Let's go."

"Not just yet," she cooed. "Daniel, this is girl talk. Why don't you go by another hot dog or something?"

"I heard that you and Daniel were together for a long time. Someone had told me that you had even been engaged right before I moved to the lake."

Meghan narrowed her eyes. "That's over."

Brittany smiled brazenly. "You're right that's over."

"Brittany, stop now." Daniel grabbed her arm and tried to pull her away but she brushed him aside like an irritating mosquito.

"Daniel told me all sorts of interesting things about you," Brittany purred. "Intimate things…"

The shock that flashed across Meghan's face was all the encouragement Brittany needed to continue her human dissection. Daniel tried to intervene again, but Brittany brushed him off. "I heard that your mother couldn't stand you, and that's why she left."

A war instantly broke out on the boardwalk. Daniel, Webster, Simon and Reid were all over Brittany like a bunch of angry bees. Meghan stood there for a moment feeling utterly speechless. When Brittany fought, she aimed to hurt deeply and that's what she had done.

Brittany was a professional at handling the offense and well as the defense in a war. She quickly side-stepped the group of boys in her face, and bent over to speak to Lindy. "Oh, you're not going to cry, are you?"

As she paused, Meghan found herself trying to frantically snap out of the trance that she had fallen into. As she looked at Brittany, she noticed her eyes weren't targeting her anymore. She followed her line of vision and gasped as she realized Brittany was targeting Lindy.

"Oh," Brittany leaned closer to Lindy, "you are going to cry. What a shame. I thought you were a big girl."

It only took a second for Meghan to identify the fact that Lindy was crying. Little tough Lindy had been scalded by sixteen-year-old Brittany's piercing words. Brittany had not only reduced Lindy to tears, she had brought her down to heart wrenching sobs that shook her entire body. Meghan had never seen Lindy cry like this in her entire life.

Meghan knelt down and took Lindy in her arms. The little girl was sobbing like her heart had been broken, and all Meghan could do was hold her for the time being. Brittany's words had found their mark on her as well, and she found herself struggling to control her own emotional tidal wave.

"You are the meanest, most self centered person I've ever met." Meghan instantly recognized Reid's voice and turned around. "I know a lot of people, Brittany and you win the prize for being the worse."

Brittany's face was covered in shock. Clearly it was not what she expected the glamour boy to say about the glamour girl.

Lindy stopped crying and poked her head around Meghan's shoulder to watch the show. "What is it, Brit? You couldn't get me, the Senator's son, so you decided to try to ruin the girl that I admire the most on the lake? Is that it? If you can't have me, then nobody can?" An audible gasp went up from Daniel. He was learning facts about his girlfriend that he didn't want to know.

Reid took another step closer to Brittany, looking much like a hunter going in for the kill. He stood there for a second, leveling her with his threatening blue eyes. "I got the messages that you called me," Reid's voice was ultra calm. "Our maid gave me all eighteen messages." He paused and was rewarded by further shock on Brittany's face. "Did it eat at you so much that I never called you back? Did you strike out at my friends because of it?"

As Reid paused again, Meghan suddenly became aware of how quiet the boardwalk had grown around them. The crowd had stopped, and people were openly staring.

"Remember, I knew well of your reputation from our days at prep school in Boston. I had heard from my friends in Boston that you were bragging about moving up here and how you would have me eating out of your hand by the end of the summer." He smiled confidently. "That's not going to happen. Not now, not ever. And," Reid's voice had dropped threateningly low, "for future reference, stay away from my family and friends. Remember, I am the Senator Kensington's son. I am well-connected, Brit. If anyone knows how to run a slanderous campaign, it's me. If you ever bother Meghan or Lindy again, I'll ruin you." Reid's face grew hard. "I'll ruin you, and I won't have to lie to do it. All I'll have to do is tell the truth about you. Your own reputation will sink you faster than anything I could ever come up with."

Everyone was shocked and completely speechless except for Reid. He leveled a look at Daniel. "Watch out Hatch. She may seem like a kitten, but she's really a serpent. You sure have gotten yourself into a real mess. Get out while you're still alive." Reid shook his head. "I don't think I'll ever understand you, Hatch. You give up the best girl on the lake for the worst. You traded in gold for plastic. The candy may be in a pretty wrapper, but it's poisoned down to the core. You have no idea what you've got, and no idea what you've lost."

Reid turned his back on Brittany and Daniel, and they scurried off like two children that had been scolded. Reid than knelt down in front of a teary-eyed Lindy. "Hey, queen," Reid spoke to Lindy gently with an unmistakable twinkle in his blue eyes, "don't you listen to the wicked witch." Lindy smiled. Reid was speaking her language. "She's just real mean, Lindy. She lies and says mean things to try to hurt people. I think she should be thrown into the deepest, darkest, stinkiest dungeon."

"Sweetbug," Meghan spoke tenderly, "Mama didn't leave us because she didn't like us." Meghan squeezed Lindy's hands. She loved this little girl so much. Meg felt the tears blind her vision. "I wish you could have seen how excited she was when you were born. I was eleven, and I remember it like it was yesterday. She really loved you so much."

"I don't remember it at all," Lindy said softly.

Reid laughed kindly and tweaked the tip of Lindy's nose. "That's because you were just a baby, Squirt. Babies don't remember when they were born."

Lindy looked at her sister thoughtfully. "Meghan, why did Mama go away? I mean, if she loved us so much, why did she leave us?"

Meghan groaned. This was not a conversation she wanted to have with Lindy on a crowded boardwalk full of people. "She had a lot of problems, Sweetie. Her problems didn't involve us at all. They were her problems. She didn't have these problems because of us. Do you understand what I'm saying Lindy?" The little girl nodded. "Mama had so many problems even before we were born." Meghan wiped her sisters tears away with her napkin. "We were the good stuff in her life, Lindy, not the bad stuff. She loved you very much."

After the girls embraced each other in a big hug, Webster put a hand on Lindy's shoulder. "Hey, Short Stuff, what do you say we go and have some fun? We have a lot of rides to go on."

Lindy shook her head. "I don't feel like going on rides. I want to go home."

"Lindy," Meghan asked quietly, "do you want to go home because of what Brittany said?"

"Yes," she admitted softly.

Meghan put an arm around Lindy's shoulders. "We came to Weir's Beach to have a good time, and I think we should. We need to go on rides and eat too much junk food and maybe win some prizes at the game booth."

Lindy looked unsure at her big sister. "Sweetbug," Meghan smiled at the long time nickname she called her little sister, "we can't let a mean liar like Brittany ruin our time. We need to go have a fun time. Come on."

"I never listen to liars," Reid admitted seriously, "especially naked liars." Reid wiggled his eyebrows at Lindy and was rewarded with a smile.

Lindy's smile grew into laughter. "She was wearing a bikini," Lindy shrugged her shoulders, "but at first, I really did think she was naked."

Reid grinned at her charmingly. "It's a really good thing that she wasn't naked because that would have been very embarrassing. Can you imagine lying naked on the dock as the Sally G. pulls up? I think I'd die!" Reid said dramatically.

Everyone laughed at the thought of it. "That's the truth!" Simon shook his head. "That would be really, really bad."

Reid took Lindy's hand in his own. "I want to go on the Ferris Wheel, but I'm afraid to go alone."

Reid looked at Lindy with big, sad, puppy-dog eyes. "Will you go with me?"

"I'll go with you," Lindy looked at him carefully, "but aren't you kind of old to be afraid of the Ferris Wheel?"

Reid laughed. "I'll tell you a secret," he whispered, "but you're going to have to promise not to tell."

Lindy's eyes lit up with excitement. An adult entrusting her with a secret was serious business. She looked absolutely honored. "I promise I won't tell."

Reid nodded. "Well, even big people get scared of things. They don't always talk about the things that they're afraid of, but they do get afraid."

"Of the Ferris Wheel?" Lindy questioned skeptically.

Reid grinned. "That's what I'm afraid of. It doesn't mean anyone else is."

Lindy nodded. " I'm afraid of some things, but I'm not afraid of the Ferris Wheel."

"Then I'd have to say you'd be the perfect person for me to ride the Ferris Wheel with." Reid paused. "What things are you afraid of?"

"Brittany," Lindy whispered.

Reid nodded and smiled at the young girl gently. "I understand why you'd be afraid of her, because she is one scary chick." Reid pushed his hair straight up and made a funny face that sent everyone around them in hysterics.

Meghan slid her hand into Lindy's. "Don't be afraid of her, Lindy. She's just a mean bully. If she ever bothers you again, I'll make her so sorry she did that she'll be afraid of us."

"Really?" Lindy questioned. "What are you going to do to her?"

Meghan laughed. "I'll think of something. Just trust me on this. OK?" Lindy nodded. "Don't be afraid. I will take care of her."

"Me too," Reid said quickly.

"And me," Simon added.

"I'm in on this, too," Web grinned. "That girl is just asking for some serious payback." Web handed Lindy a pink cotton candy. "I've been looking for an excuse to take care of her since I met her. Don't worry, Lindy. You have a whole team of people ready to do battle for you."

As they made their way to the Ferris Wheel, Meghan couldn't help but wonder what Reid Kensington was up to. He never wanted to be part of their group before. It wasn't as if he ignored her in the past, it was just that he never went out of his way to be around her. He was always nice to her, but this was the first time that the Perfect Prince had sought her out. And, if that wasn't enough, he was fighting her battles for her as if he had done it all his life. It was nice, but weird at the same time. She knew it was going to take some serious thinking to even attempt to figure him out.

As they got on the Ferris Wheel together, Lindy sandwiched herself in between Meghan and the young Robert Redford look alike. Meghan glanced quickly at Reid, trying not to stare. He was absolutely gorgeous. Why in the world would someone that looked like that want to have anything to do with her. It didn't make any sense. She caught Simon's eye. He wasn't volunteering any clues about the situation. She'd plug him later for answers. This was all too strange.

Meghan, Lindy, Reid, Simon and Web went on all the rides together. Meghan felt a certain amount of satisfaction knowing she had gone on the rides and survived them. This was the first year she didn't get sick on something or someone.

When they stopped at a booth to get some hot fudge sundaes, Web starting acting stranger than normal. "Oh, no," he jumped behind Meghan, "oh, hide me. Please, you've got to hide me."

"Web," Meghan turned to look at her friend, "what are you doing?"

"Don't say my name out loud!" he pleaded. "I don't want her to know I'm here."

"Who?" Simon was scanning the area for possible monsters or alien sightings. "What's with you, man?"

That's when Meghan spotted Natasha North coming toward them. "Web," Meghan said compassionately, "as I see it, you have two choices to make. You can either shoot yourself or you can try to act normal around her for once. You're acting like a two-year-old."

"Oh, shoot me!" Web begged. "I can't handle being around her. I make a fool of myself every time."

Meghan laughed. "I don't want to be the first one to tell you this, but you're making a fool of yourself right now."

"You see what she does to me?" Web's eyes bugged out. "It's awful."

"Web," Meghan tired to reason with her friend who was on the border of sheer panic, "Natasha's really nice. You should try to talk to her."

"Are you kidding? She's a girl! I can't talk to her."

Meghan laughed. "I'm glad you know she's a girl, Web, and I'm not trying to stress you out even more, but here's a news flash for you, so am I."

"I know that," Web muttered.

"Uh, she's coming straight toward us," Reid warned. "You'd better either shape up or ship out."

"Hide me, Simon!" Webster was so pathetic you couldn't help but take pity on him.

"Come with me." Simon grabbed Web's arm and took him around the back of the ice cream sundae booth to hide. Reid followed, shaking his head in disbelief. He had never hid from a girl in all his life. He couldn't relate to Web's turmoil.

As Natasha approached the group, only Meghan and Lindy remained. "Hi, Natasha," Meg greeted her warmly, "how are you doing?"

"Great," Natasha looked around curiously. "I love living on the lake. It's so peaceful and quiet." She paused and glanced around again. "Did I just see Webster here?"

Meghan smiled. "He had to go."

"Is he coming back?" Natasha asked hopefully.

Meg smiled. Web would probably have an all out heart attack if he knew that Natasha was interested in him. "I'm not sure," Meghan answered honestly. She was trying her best to save Web's dignity. He had fallen for Natasha hard, and it was making him fall apart.

"Tell him I said hi," Nat was still scanning the area for him.

"I will," Meghan smiled again. Just that simple message might put Web over the edge.

"Hey, do you want to get together sometime?"

"I'd love to. I work a lot, but you could always ride the water taxi with me and keep me company. Simon and Web ride with me several times a week just to catch up on things."

Natasha smiled. "I would love to ride with you, especially if Webster was riding along. Does he ride on a certain day?"

Meghan shrugged. "I'll have to get back to you on that." She wouldn't consciously give Web a heart attack. "I could swing by Indian Island and pick you up. Every Monday I go by your stop around ten."

Nat smiled, and Meghan knew in an instant that they were going to be good friends. Natasha was genuine and kind and lots of fun to be with.

"I would love to ride with you, Meghan. Maybe you can help me learn the lake better." Natasha laughed. "I took daddy's boat out last week and got lost trying to find my way home. Some of these islands look so much the same to me."

Meghan smiled. "That's true. It does take time to distinguish between them. You'll eventually find that they take on personalities of their own. Like your island," Meghan gestured with her hand, "Indian Island is easy to find because it has a very tall tree at the north end of the island. It always reminded me of a feather in an Indian's hat."

Natasha's eyes lit up with understanding. "Hey, I know the tree you're talking about. It does look like an Indian feather."

"You'll get to know the islands after time, and they'll become like old friends to you."

"I can already see that," Nat smiled. "Well, I should be going. This is a father/daughter date night, and I promised my dad that I'd go on the roller coaster with him."

"Sounds fun," Meg smiled. "I'll see you Monday."

Right after Natasha left, Simon, Reid, and a very shaken looking Webster appeared from behind the ice cream stand. "Did you have to go on all day talking and talking to her?" Web whined. "Have you no mercy on my situation at all?"

Meghan laughed. "Exactly what is your situation?"

Web sighed loudly. "I am a victim of male, teenage hormones. I don't want to like girls, especially after what happened with you and Daniel, but I don't seem to have a choice in the matter. My hormones are dragging me toward her, and I'm being completely tortured."

"Do you feel like you're walking the plank, Web?" Reid asked.

"As a matter of fact I do and under the plank are a thousand hungry alligators arguing over who's going to get to eat me."

"You have watched too much Peter Pan," Meghan laughed.

"You have no idea what I'm going through," Web grumbled.

"I guess this wouldn't be the time to tell you that Natasha North," Meghan touched Web's arm, "by the way, that is her name."

"I know her name," Web stated impatiently. "What about her?"

"You don't have to talk about her like she's some kind of virus."

"I'd rather have a virus. At least I know I'd get over that. Oh, man," Web groaned, "she's the most beautiful girl that I've ever seen." Web paused and looked at Meghan. "Uh, next to you, of course."

Meghan laughed. "Of course."

"Don't you think she's beautiful?"

Meghan nodded. "She's beautiful, and she's very kind."

"Oh, I'm not going to stand a chance if she's both beautiful and kind." Web grabbed Meghan by the shoulders. "Are you sure she's kind? Maybe she's just putting on a show?"

Meghan laughed. "Not only is she kind, she's interested in you."

"No…" Web said the word as if he had just been handed a death sentence. "I'm doomed."

"Hang in there, buddy," Simon tired to encouraged his friend, "I'll stand with you through thick and thin."

"You're a true friend, man," Web said the words gratefully.

As the evening wrapped up, the five of them made their way to their boats. Reid pulled Meghan aside for a moment. "What time does church start tomorrow?"

Meghan stared at Reid a moment before answering. "I've never seen you there before."

Reid laughed. "That's why I need to know what time church starts."

"It starts at nine." Meghan watched him carefully. She still hadn't figured out whatever it was that he was up to.

Reid nodded and took Meghan's hand and held it gently for a second. "Thank you for letting me hang out with you tonight. I know you don't trust me, Meghan, but I'm not the same jerk that I used to be."

"I never thought you were a jerk," Meg whispered.

"I was," Reid nodded seriously. "I had my priorities all messed up. I'm changing, Meghan and I want you to be a part of that change." He smiled at her, handed her a long stemmed rose and then jogged off toward his boat.

As Meghan watched him go, in stunned silence, she also saw Daniel Hatch on the far end of the dock staring at her. He was standing by himself, and by the serious expression that covered his face, Meg was pretty sure that he had just seen the whole interlude between her and Reid. They stared at each other for a minute, without saying a word. The tender way Daniel looked at her made her want to cry. As he spotted the red rose, he slowly shook his head and then turned and left.

As Meghan stared at the empty dock before her two things ran through her mind. Why had Daniel come to see her? Had he come to apology for his nasty girlfriend or was there something else? She hated the fact that she could still see the love he had for her in his brown eyes. Why was it there if he was dating Brittany? He had no right to look at her like that.

As Meghan looked at the beautiful, long-stemmed rose in her hands, her eyes narrowed thoughtfully. What in the world was Reid Kensington up to? What had possessed him to give her a red rose, and why did he suddenly want her to be part of the change in his life? Too much was happening with the men in her life and right at the moment, none of it made sense.

Thirteen

The cove at Alton Bay was packed with boaters Sunday morning to hear the weekly open-air sermon by the lake. As Meghan pulled her water taxi into the bay, she noticed Simon and Reid.

"Simon's over there." Lindy waved to him.

Meghan nodded. So is Reid, she thought curiously. Why the sudden interest in church now? What was happening in his life that would want to make the Perfect Prince come to church? She tried not to stare at him but found it difficult.

As the opening songs were beginning to be sung, Reid glanced over at Meghan and waved. Meghan noticed a black Bible in his lap. She sighed. She didn't even know that he owned a Bible.

"Hi, Reid!" Lindy shouted across the bay. Meghan cringed as all the boaters around stared at Lindy and Reid. Reid handled the attention graciously. He smiled at Lindy and gave her a little wave, and then directed his attention back to the singing.

Meghan stole quick glances at Reid throughout the service. He appeared to be genuinely interested in what the pastor was saying and followed along in his Bible diligently.

Today's guest speaker was a pastor from Maine. Pastor Allen was speaking on expectations. "How many of you out there know what God's will is for your life?" A few hands went up.

"I bet a lot of you know what the will or expectation is of those around you." People were nodding and a man in the boat next to Meg groaned loudly.

"How many of you know what it's like to carry the hopes, dreams and expectations of others on your back?" Almost everyone's hand went up. "It can be an incredibly heavy load for a person to carry the expectations of others with them. I find it completely draining and totally exhausting. The pressure is on. They love you, believe in you, and almost demand that you succeed. They place you high on a pedestal and turn you into their personal Superman. You soon find out what a very lonely place the top can be. You're not allowed to have problems or difficulties in your life, and to ever fail at anything is completely out of the question. You can't fail them. You're their Superman. They don't want you to have problems. They want you to have the perfect life that they're not able to have." The pastor paused thoughtfully. "My friend, no one is perfect but God, and only He can live a perfect life. Being Superman is a role that a mere mortal can succeed in, because it's a role that you weren't meant to play."

Pastor Allen scanned the crowd of boaters thoughtfully. "How many of you have known the agony of defeat when you fail? How many of you know what it's like to disappoint the same group of people that have turned you into Superman?" Many hands went up.

"How many of you know the agony of defeat when these well-meaning people that turned you into Superman in the first place kick you off the pedestal? They face you day after day with the quiet look of hurt and disappointment that only falling off the pedestal can bring."

"To disappoint the same group of people who believed in you is one of the most awful feelings I know." Pastor Allen paused. "It's like a slow torture, a slow death, and the pain runs deeper than a physical wound. You pray for it to be over quickly, but the aftermath of the disappointment rides on and on."

Meghan could see that many of the people were agreeing with the pastor's words. She glanced over at Simon and Reid and was surprised to find Reid slumped over with Simon's arm around him. Once again, Meghan tried not to stare. What in the world did the great Reid Kensington have to feel bad about? He was the golden boy, the chosen one to take over his father's political legacy. All the guys on the lake wanted to be him, and all the girls on the lake wanted to date him. Meghan smiled. It sounded like a dream come true.

Pastor Allen, continued and Meghan forced herself to concentrate on the sermon again. "Once you fall off the pedestal, you begin to learn a new feeling. The feeling is not a pleasant one. What overwhelms you is a feeling of loss and inadequacy. It's a terrible feeling when no one believes in you or has confidence in you. As you try to pick up the pieces of your life and go on, a lonely, cold feeling of abandonment washes over you as you realize that the people who once made you Superman don't have the faith in you to believe you can do anything right anymore."

Pastor Allen paused thoughtfully. "I don't know about you, but I don't want to be on anyone's pedestal or be anyone's Superman. I can't fly and I can't save them, only God can. You see, that's the key. They should be looking to God to carry them through life's tough times. God is the only one that can save them, and God is the only one that should be placed on the pedestal. God alone belongs on the throne, and it's very unfair of people when they take God off the throne and place you up there instead. They have destined you for failure without you even knowing it. They believe you should be able to perform the way God does; and the major problem with that is that you can't and never will be able to because you're not God. Only God is God."

Pastor Allen cleared his throat and then continued. "We must look to God. Each one of us must put God on the throne. Don't put your family there or your friends there. If you do, you're only taking God away from his rightful position and setting up your family and friends for ultimate failure. Trust in Him. Turn to Him. Whether you're at the top of the ladder or the bottom, or someplace in between, turn to God and He will never let you down. He will give you the strength to live each day and meet each day's challenges."

After the sermon ended, the boats slowly began to pull away. Meghan noticed right away that Reid and Simon stayed behind. They appeared to be in quiet a heated discussion. Reid got behind the wheel of his boat and pulled it up to the dock, and then he and Simon went over to talk to Pastor Allen.

Meghan had to leave to bring her seniors back to their various islands. As she glanced back one last time, she saw Reid talking to Pastor Allen. What was going on with the Perfect Prince? She'd have to talk to Simon. It was one more thing on the list that she wanted to know about his older brother.

She found that she didn't have to wait long. Later that same evening, Simon and Reid entered Penny's

Cove on black jet skis and came right up to Meghan's dock. "Do you feel like a little company?" Reid was unusually serious.

"Sure." Meghan had been playing a game of Parcheesi with Lindy on the dock. The little bug had set up block-ades all over the board and Meghan found herself more than ready to quit. "We'll finish this later," Meghan grinned knowing they never would.

Lindy nodded reluctantly. "Can I go over and see Aunt Birdie? She said she was going to be mak-ing cookies this afternoon, and I want to help."

Meghan laughed as Snacks popped out of a deep, snoring sleep at the sound of the word cookie. The Springer Spaniel looked at Meghan expectantly. "I didn't say it."

The dog then diverted her attention to Lindy. "I'll bring Snacks, too. We'll both help Aunt Birdie make cookies."

Meagan smiled. What Lindy had failed to say was that she wanted to help eat the cookies. The only part of the cooking process that Lindy liked was the consumption part. "Don't eat too many cookies. Last time you helped her with cookies you came home sick." Lindy scowled. "And don't feed any to Snacks. You know she gets awful gas when you do. We'll be tortured tonight as she explodes." Lindy frowned. "You know Snacks is lethal when she eats people food. Take some dog cookies with you." Lindy nodded and then ran off in the direction of Aunt Birdie's cottage with Snacks close at her heels.

Meghan turned her attention back to her friends and didn't have to wait very long for the discussion to begin. "I want to talk to you about something that happened today." Something caught Reid's attention out of the corner of his eye, and he turned to see Daniel and Webster standing on the Hatch dock. "Hey, guys, come over and join us."

As Daniel and Web swam across the small cove, Meghan's curiosity about what Reid wanted to share with her rose big time. Reid turned to Meg. "I'd like them to hear this too." Meghan nodded and hoped they swam fast.

When Daniel and Web climbed onto the Kane's dock, Meghan threw some towels at them. "Thanks for coming," Reid looked at each of the guys. "Something happened today and I'd like you to hear it from me." Reid blew out a loud breath. "The way rumors circulate around the lake, I figure that if you get the story from me, I'll know that you're hearing it straight." Everyone looked at Reid interestedly.

"I went to church with Simon this morning. He's been inviting me for years, but I basically thought that church was only for losers." He paused and looked apologetically at the group around him. Everyone on the dock went to church on a regular basis. "I regret my attitude. I was wrong."

He paused again and seemed to be struggling for the right words. Meghan bit back her shock. Reid had always been such a natural spokesperson. He could charm an audience with grace and sincerity whether he was genuine about what he was saying or not.

"Pastor Allen from Maine was preaching today at Alton Bay. He spoke about what it's like to have people's expectations on you. I could really relate to this, because my own path was chosen for me before I was even born. I have been carrying around the expectations of others all my life. Being the oldest Kensington, I was expected to follow in the footsteps of my father. I was the male heir to his political throne. My father and his people groomed me for political life as a young boy." Reid sighed. "I was never asked what I wanted to do with my life. They had already made the decision for me, and I was trained for the job from a very young age."

Reid ran a hand through his blonde hair anxiously. "You guys have no idea the amount of pressure I was under. Simon could see it, and he often helped me deal with it." Reid laid a hand on his brother's back. "Simon was the one who was always there for me and quite honestly, kept me from cracking time and time again."

Reid exhaled loudly. "I've done a lot of things that I regret. Some of it was from the pressure, and some of it was my own foolishness. When everyone you know is telling you how wonderful you are, somewhere along the way you start to believe it yourself."

Reid looked at Meghan. "I originally wanted to come to church to impress you." Daniel's eyebrows flew up. "Once I got there, I felt that the pastor was speaking just to me and that initial attitude changed very quickly."

Reid sighed again. "I don't think any of you have any idea how much pressure it is to be the Senator's son. Everyone expects so much from Simon and I that I often felt like I was drowning. I was trying so hard to reach those unattainable goals that others set for me that I completely lost sight of who I was and what I wanted to be." He shook his head sadly. "I got to the point that I didn't know who I was anymore. I felt like a puppet for my father. I was a walking tape recorder, spouting off his ideas and not my own."

Reid looked thoughtfully at the group that he hoped would someday soon become his friends. "I can see that I've shocked you. Just imagine the shock that my father is going to feel when I talk to him." Both Reid and Simon laughed. "Hang on, because you haven't heard the best yet. Simon and I stayed after the service to talk with Pastor Allen. We talked to him for three hours and he patiently answered all my questions." Reid's face lit up. "I finally understand what Simon has been talking about for years. I gave my heart to Christ today. I became a Christian."

The silence on the dock was deafening. Web was the first one to respond. "Man, congratulations. That's great! I never thought I'd lived to see the day that you became saved." He gave Reid a big hug and then grinned. "Man, now there's hope for everyone."

Everyone laughed. 'You're right Web. If God can save the Perfect Prince then He can save anyone."

Daniel stuck his hand out formally and Reid shook it. "I'm happy for you."

Daniel hesitated and Reid picked up on it right away. "You don't believe me." It was a statement not a question.

"I'm not a judge, Reid," Daniel answered evenly.

Reid smiled. "But you're judging me, Hatch. I can see it in your eyes. I'm not winning your vote of approval."

"Do you need it?" Daniel asked defiantly.

"No," Reid answered honestly, "but I'd like it."

"You have quite a reputation."

"That's going to be my cross to carry, Hatch. I've done a lot of stupid things in the past. Right now, all I'm asking is that you give me the benefit of the doubt. I realize a lot of people are not going to believe that I've changed. Hopefully," Reid shrugged, "in time they will see that I have."

"Tell me," Daniel threw his hands on his hips defensively, "why would a rich prince like you think he needs God?"

"I'll tell you why," Reid answered directly. "I've lived a very privileged life. With my father's political positions and my family's wealth, I got to experience many things that the average person never will. I'm only eighteen, and I've got to live a life that most people would only dream of." Reid paused and took a step closer to Daniel. "Do you know what all this high stakes living has taught me?"

"I have no idea," Daniel replied evenly.

"That even though I had everything that money could buy, I was very lonely and miserable inside. You can't buy happiness. No matter how much money you have or how much you spend, happiness isn't for sale. You know what else you can't buy?"

"What?"

"You can't buy love, and you certainly can't buy salvation. Only God can save us, and only he can set us free." He stared at Daniel hard. "I've tried all the toys, Hatch. They're exciting when you first get them but after the shine wears off, I'm still the same empty, lonely person that I was before. Don't be fooled by the things money can buy. That's all they are—things. Nothing gives you peace in your heart like God does." Reid paused. "I wish I could make you understand the fact that for the first time in my life I have peace in my heart. I've been trying to get this feeling for a long time Hatch. Now I've got it, no one is going to ever take it away."

Daniel clapped his hands together mocking Reid. "Nice speech, Senator. You always knew how to deliver a line."

"Daniel," Reid eyed the teen closely, "I wasn't giving a speech. I was sharing my salvation story with you. People change, Daniel. Both you and I are living proof of that fact. I've changed, and so have you. You're not the same guy you were two months ago. Watch out Hatch, Brittany is taking you down the drain with her."

Daniel grinned sarcastically. "Here you don't want me judging you, and I find that as soon as you can, you're judging me. That doesn't seem right. It seems kind of hypocritical to me."

Reid nodded. "To some maybe, but there is one huge difference. I've confessed my sin to God. Brittany Bentley hasn't ever been sorry for anything in her life."

"It seems a bit hard, Reid."

"That's because I know facts about her that you don't."

"What are you talking about?" Daniel was getting heated.

"I don't think that you're really interested in the facts, Hatch. I've tried to tell you before, but you never listened."

"I'm listening now."

"Brittany's life in Boston makes me look like a saint. She's been sleeping around since she was twelve and has had four abortions that I personally know of."

"I don't believe you."

Reid shook his head sadly. "I couldn't make this up if I wanted to. She uses people and manipulates them for her own benefit. She leaves a long line of hurting people in her wake."

"How do I know you're telling the truth?"

"We went to the same prep school in Boston since kindergarten. Simon was actually in Brittany's grade. He can verify everything I'm saying."

"He's telling the truth, Daniel," Simon admitted quietly. "Brittany would often come up to our room and dump her problems on us. Her problems were always real enough, but I always felt that she was trying to get any kind of attention that she could get from Reid. She's been after him for as long as I can remember." Simon sighed. "She never tried to hide the fact that she was after the Senator's son. She wanted to be in the spotlight, and she saw Reid as her ticket to do that."

Daniel exhaled loudly. Maybe he didn't believe Reid, but he had known Simon too long not to believe him. Since childhood, Simon had never exaggerated facts or stories, he simply told the truth. Simon was too pure to even think of lying.

"I'm sorry, Daniel," Simon laid a hand on his friend's shoulder. "I tried to tell you before, but you didn't listen. She's bad news. You should get away from her as fast as you can."

Reid nodded. "Get away from her, Hatch. She's evil. She will eat you up and spit you out and never think of you again."

Daniel sighed. "I've got to go." He dove into the water, and Meghan sadly watched him swim back to his side of Penny's Cove. She could see the struggle within him against what he knew to be true and what he wanted to believe was true.

How incredibly ironic, Meghan thought sadly. The one man she thought would never come to the Lord just did, and the one man she thought would never walk away from the Lord just had. She shook her head feeling miserable inside. Life was something that no one could predict, and people's choices were another thing that you couldn't forecast. You couldn't always guess what they would do with their life. After watching what had happened to both Reid and Daniel, she felt more certain than ever that life was very unpredictable.

Fourteen

"*D*id you hear who the latest victim was?" Roy asked the planning committee heatedly. They looked at him with blank expressions. "Miss Perty! Can you believe those boys would aim their garbage shooting cannon at an eighty- nine -year old lady?"

"That's awful!" Meghan was appalled. Miss Perty was one of her regulars on the water taxi. She was a sweet little old lady that liked to bake her and Lindy cookies and knit them scarves in the winter. The idea of Miss Perty cover with rotten vegetable garbage made Meghan's blood boil.

"Something has to be done," Simon looked at the group fiercely.

"It's past time," Reid admitted. "Those juvenile delinquents need to start reaping what they've been shooting at us for so long."

"I've named the mission, Operation Vegetation." Everyone laughed. "Now we need a plan." Web eyed the group eagerly. "Does anyone have any ideas?" Web laughed. "I have had several plans, but my dad keeps telling me that they're too violent."

"Like what? Reid asked curiously.

"I wanted to throw them off their tree forts with concrete blocks tied to their feet." Everyone laughed. Considering the fact that they were talking about the Baker boys, the idea did have a certain appeal.

"That's too violent," Reid laughed. "Tempting," he grinned at Web, "but definitely too violent."

"My dad made me solemnly promise that I wouldn't do anything that would get me thrown in jail." Daniel laughed. "He's afraid the college admission-department might frown on a freshman with a criminal record." More laughter floated through the air.

"We're not going to do anything that's going to get you thrown in the clink," Ray laughed. "One of the proudest achievements that Roy and I have come up with is to transform Simon's paintball gun into a veggie gun. It can now shoot tomatoes instead of paint balls."

The kids looked at the older brother's with new admiration. "How did you manage that?" Daniel asked clearly impressed.

Roy laughed. "I put my scientific background to good use."

Ray grinned. "A scientific mind is a terrible thing to waste."

The kids laughed. The Hobson brothers knew how to have fun. Their ideas for this event were creative and innovative.

"A standard paintball gun can shoot all kinds of interesting things," Ray's eyes gleamed. "It doesn't take much imagination to think about what you can stuff in there."

"It's a very versatile piece of equipment," Roy added.

"I was thinking that we could use their pulley system against them," Web smiled. "That way we can haul up all the rotten ammo that we want." Web laughed. "I think I've had far too long to think about this. We could even dress up in black outfits with gas masks."

Simon shook his head. "Gas masks scare me."

"You're scared of your own shadow," Web teased.

"That's true," Simon grinned, "so you can just imagine what a gas mask will do to a guy like me."

"OK," Web nodded, "no gas masks."

"I have an idea for Operation Vegetation," Daniel grinned. Planning what you wanted to do to the Triple Trouble was a lot of fun. "Mr. Eddy, who works on the mail boat with my dad, is a volunteer fireman on the lake. I heard him telling my dad that the firemen are looking for a house to practice their maneuvers on."

"What maneuvers?" Meg asked curiously.

"They are looking for someone to volunteer their house to get plastered with water. They don't need to put out an actual fire, they just like to check their hoses and lines every once in a while to make sure everything is working properly."

Reid laughed. "They're just looking for an excuse to play fireman. I've watched those volunteers. They're good and all, but they're really just big kids at heart. They've graduated from Super Soakers to the fireboat."

"It does look like a lot of fun," Daniel smiled. "I'm thinking of joining them in a few years."

Roy looked thoughtful. "Well, we're off to a good start. We can use the paintball guns to shoot the veggie compost, and the fireboat can hose them off when we're done." He paused. "I still feel like we need a little more."

"What else have those boys shot at people?" Roy asked his accomplishes.

"Eggs," Simon and Meghan said in unison.

"And the reason that you know this?" Roy chuckled.

"Those little brats bombed my taxi with eggs one day." Meghan shook her head. Even though it had happened over a month ago, she was still mad. "Simon happened to be on board, and he got creamed."

Daniel laughed, and Meg stared at him for a second. He was acting like the old, easygoing Daniel that she had grown up with and loved. Meghan smiled. Even if it was only for a moment, she'd enjoy it. She silently prayed for Daniel to return to his normal self again. She missed the old Daniel. She didn't miss Daniel her boyfriend, but she missed Daniel, her friend. Daniel smiled at her for a moment. She knew he was struggling with a lot of issues, and she hoped his issues didn't drown him. She found herself praying for him once again that he'd give his heart back to God. If he tried to sort through life's messes on his own, she was afraid that he wasn't gong to make it.

Daniel sighed and turned his attention back to the group. "They also use a potato gun. They load it with dozens of eggs." He laughed. "On the Sally G. one day, I must have gotten hit with over three dozen eggs." He laughed again. "I never saw it coming. What a mess that was. My dad tossed me into the lake to clean up."

"You know, my sister Grace has a potato gun," Roy said thoughtfully. "She uses it to chase the crows out of her garden." He looked at his brother. "I never thought of filling the thing with eggs."

"It could be pretty interesting," Ray smiled.

"I think you're right." Roy laughed. "I'm sure Gracie would volunteer the gun for the mission."

"She's so mad at them that I think she'd volunteer the eggs, too." Ray shook his head. "She's been the victim of their shenanigans for years."

"Lindy is going to want in on this," Meghan's voice was thoughtful. "They ruined her queen outfit with rotten tomatoes and eggs."

"She could man the water balloon sling shot," Web grinned. "That should make up for some of her loss."

"She'd love to do that," Meghan nodded excitedly.

As the plans for the attack fell into place, there was already a taste of sweet victory floating through the air. This job was long overdue and all the participants involved were more than willing to do their part.

Phase One of Operation Vegetation would have Meghan, Lindy, Roy and Ray Hobson serving as decoys. They would enter Pirates Cove, as if Meghan were taxiing the Hobson brothers and try to act as normal as possible. Once the war got under way, the four of them would man a giant water balloon slingshot from the boat. They would prepare the balloons ahead of time, filling the entire bottom of the boat with them. They would throw a tarp from the marina over the top of them to disguise them.

Phase Two of the mission would begin the same as Phase one. As Meghan's taxi entered Pirates Cove, Daniel, Reid, Simon and Web would enter the Baker's tree fort from the north side of the island. The woods behind the tree fort would serve as a great camouflage to enter and exit the fort.

Web would operate the potato gun with plenty of rotten veggies for ammo. Simon and Reid would use their paintball guns and fill them with the same ammo that Web was using.

Phase Three would begin upon the completion of Phase Two. The fireboat would enter Pirates Cove and hose the boys down thoroughly. They felt that cleaning the boys up was the least they could do after plastering the boys with veggies.

Phase Four would find the men dressed in black, returning to the fort, and having a nice little heart-to-heart talk with the Baker boys. The boys needed to understand that if anyone on the lake complained of getting bombed by them again, they would be back and next time would be much worse.

Operation Vegetation went off without a hitch. The Baker boys were scared stiff by the ammo they shot at others coming back at them. When the tables were turned around on them, they didn't like getting their own medicine one bit.

The group felt confident that boaters would now be able to pass by the Baker boy's tree fort without incident. Reid said he wouldn't go so far to say they had reformed the boys, they had simply refocused them. If someone got hit, they knew it would come back to them twice fold. Suddenly, the idea of bombing the boaters didn't seem to be quite as appealing. All the lake would thank them.

Fifteen

$\mathscr{A}$s Meghan pulled her water taxi up to Gumdrop Island town dock, she cringed inside as she looked back and saw the Sally G. right behind her. There was no way to avoid seeing Daniel. The U.S. Mail Boat would be docked right behind her in a matter of minutes.

Mr. Hatch sounded the air horn on the Sally G., and many of the island children that were near the docks came running to greet the boat. It was always an event when the mail boat pulled up to any island. The adults longed for news from the mainland and looked forward to getting their mail. The kids, on the other hand, were waiting to see Daniel Hatch. Daniel ran the snack bar aboard the mail boat and every day when the Sally G. pulled up to the islands, the kids raced to see Daniel and get their daily supply of candy.

Meghan smiled as she watched the kids crowd onto the Sally G. They would keep Daniel busy for quite a while. Hopefully she would get all her passengers loaded before Daniel was done serving the kids.

Meghan smiled as old Mr. Duffy climbed on board. Lindy greeted him, shook his hand and then collected the fare. He turned to find Meghan and waved at her. He always got such a kick out Lindy. Most people did. She was a character and knew how to have fun with her job.

As Meghan steered her boat toward Lollipop Island, she glanced down at her roster. She had to pick up three seniors and drop off Mr. Duffy so he could visit his elderly sister. Meghan smiled. Mr. Duffy was ninety-one. He didn't consider himself elderly because his sister was ninety-six.

Once they docked at Lollipop Island, the three passengers waiting for the taxi quickly boarded. Meghan felt her stomach knot as she heard the sound of the Sally G. pulling in behind her. She knew that her chances were not good that old Mr. Duffy would move quickly enough for her to get away a second time.

Mr. Hatch sounded his air horn and as if on cue, all the kids come running for his boat. They were well trained and fast. Meghan had to smile. Whenever candy was involved, kids moved with lightning speed.

As Meghan was watching Lindy take the fare from the new passengers, Daniel suddenly appeared at her side. She looked at him in shock. "How did you get away from all those kids?"

Daniel laughed. "Dad offered to take the snack bar for me so I could talk to you. I tried to catch you at Gumdrop, but I had too many kids at the snack bar."

Meghan smiled. "I just thought the Sally G. was going to follow me around the lake the whole day."

"I thought I might have to so I could talk to you."

Meghan studied him a minute. "What's up?" she asked hesitantly. She tried to sound casual, but she felt anything but casual. Daniel always found a way to reach deep down to her heart. Even after they had broken up, she still felt too many spinning emotions around him. It left her feeling tense and uneasy.

So much had changed between them; yet in some ways, nothing had changed at all. They had known each other all their lives and along with that amount of time comes a great deal of knowledge. They knew each other's strengths and weaknesses. They knew each other's dreams and desires. It was far more personal than she ever wanted to be with Daniel again.

As she glanced at Daniel as he stood along side of her boat, she desperately wished that he no longer knew so much about her. Now that they weren't dating anymore, what had once been thought of as privileged information was now something Meg thought of as an invasion of privacy. She suddenly felt very exposed.

"I've been wanting to talk to you for a while." Daniel jarred her mind from her thoughts. "I feel like we never get to see each other anymore."

Meghan laughed. "That's because we don't." She didn't add the fact that it was also fine with her. Generally when two people broke up, they didn't see each other anymore. What was Daniel up to? His rejection, as much as she hated to admit it, still stung deeply.

"How's Brittany doing?" Meghan asked in an icy tone.

Daniel's eyes narrowed. "Fine." He didn't expanded; he just continued to stare at her in a way that angered her.

"So, are you still dating her?"

"Yes," Daniel answered in a reserved way.

"So, all that stuff that Simon and Reid told you didn't make any difference to you?"

"God wants us to forgive, Meg," Daniel stared at her hard for a second and she felt herself flinch. When he looked at her that way, she always felt like he could see right through her. It annoyed her to no end.

Her anger fueled her conversation. "There's a difference between forgiveness and being involved with someone who's still actively pursuing a life that is far from God."

"Yes, there is," Daniel stated defensively. "What you failed to see is the fact that Brittany has changed."

Daniel softened. "She shouldn't have said what she said. I'm sorry about that."

"You have nothing to be sorry for. As for Brittany, I don't see her ever apologizing to me or Lindy. You know," Meghan couldn't hold her anger back, "it wasn't that long ago that you would have pounded someone for speaking to Lindy and me that way." Meghan looked up at Daniel with hurt radiating from her eyes. "You used to care, Daniel. Brittany hasn't changed, but you have. If Reid hadn't stepped in, I don't know what would have happened."

"Reid," Daniel muttered his name with distain.

"I'm glad that Reid was on the boardwalk that night. He was a gentleman, and he stood up for me and Lindy."

"And he gave you a red rose," Daniel's voice was accusing.

Meghan tried to hide her shock. She wasn't sure if he had noticed the rose. Now that question had been answered. "He was being nice."

"He's after you," Daniel spat out angrily. "Now you have both of the Senator's sons after you."

"What are you talking about?"

Daniel's laugh came out sounding cold and mean. "Simon has been after you for years. You didn't see it then and you probably don't see it now. He's always liked you."

"He's one of my best friends."

Daniel nodded. "He's a friend that has been a little in love with you for years." Daniel shook his head. "I often felt like I was competing with Simon for your attention."

Meghan turned away for a second. She did not want to hear this. She wanted Simon to stay safely in the friendship category. She knew in her heart that she could never love Simon more than a brother.

Meghan looked at Daniel and her eyes narrowed. She shook her head as a new understanding to an old situation suddenly made things very clear for her. "Is that why you did it?"

"Did what?" Daniel seemed clueless, but Meghan was on to him.

"Is that why you gave me an engagement ring? Where you afraid that Simon might ask me before you did?"

"No." Daniel's face was bathed in guilt, and Meghan knew she was onto something that she didn't really want to know.

"You never really wanted to get engaged, did you?" Meghan stepped out of her boat and onto the dock. "You were just putting me on reserve in case you decided that you wanted to go in that direction down the road." She threw an angry finger in his chest. "You wanted to make sure no one else could have me while you took your time making up your mind about the situation." Meghan brushed back a tear that began falling down her check. "I can't believe I was so blind!"

"I'm really sorry, Meg," Daniel dug his toe into the dock. "I never thought things would turn out this way."

"I bet you didn't." Meghan eyed him accusingly. "While I was dreaming of marriage and kids, you were putting me on hold, and I didn't even know it."

"It's really not like that."

"It's exactly like that." As she looked into his eyes they told her the truth that she didn't want to hear. He had been biding his time, making up his mind while she thought they were on their way to the altar. "I can't believe this! I feel so stupid. You used me, and I didn't even have a clue."

As Meghan turned to get back into her boat, Daniel touched her arm to stop her. "That's not true. Wait," he pleaded, "I wanted to tell you to be careful around Reid. I'm not convinced he's really changed."

"Judging people, are you, Daniel?"

"Just observing," he shot back.

"For the record," Meghan threw her hands on her hips, "I think Reid has changed. He's different and," she took a step closer to him, "so are you. You've changed Daniel, and it's not for the better."

As Meghan started her boat she felt like she couldn't get away from Daniel fast enough. Things had changed. The romantic fairy tale was over, and it did not end happily ever after. Knowing that Daniel had put her on reserve as far as marriage really angered her and hurt her deeply. How could he do such a thing?

Meghan slowly shook her head. She was beginning to question everything that she had with Daniel. She didn't know what had really been real and what had only been real in her mind. How much of the fairy tale had they shared together? How much of it had been a one-way street? As she shut her eyes for a minute, she shook her head. How on earth could she have been so blind? At that moment, she didn't know if she would ever trust another guy in her life. Meghan sighed. She knew she didn't want to. She didn't want to ever open up her heart to getting trampled again. It wasn't worth it. When all the pieces came crashing down, the pain outweighed anything good. Guys would be off limits to her for a very long time, even if they were the Senator's sons. No one was gaining entrance to her heart again for a very long time. It just wasn't worth it.

Sixteen

*S*unday was fast becoming Meghan's favorite day of the week. She looked forward to the waterside service at Alton Bay. As soon as it ended, she found herself anticipating next week's service.

This week, the speaker was Pastor Sherman from Vermont. As the opening songs were being sung, Meghan immediately spotted Simon and Reid on one side of her and Webster, sitting with his father and grandmother on the other side of her. Natasha North, who was sitting in front of her, turned around and waved.

Over the course of the summer, Meghan was beginning to value Nat's friendship quite a lot. Natasha was the first girlfriend that Meghan ever had. Growing up on Lake Winnipesaukee with all boys had been lonely at times. It was nice to have someone to discuss girl issues with that really understood girl issues.

As Meghan scanned Alton Bay, she spotted Mr. and Mrs. Hatch. Her heart sunk as she saw that Daniel was once again not with them. Meghan didn't get it. How could someone who was once such a strong Christian change so much from what they had once been? It was as if Daniel had almost entirely left his Christian identity and traded it in for a very worldly way. She prayed that he would come back to the Daniel that he once was.

Meghan sighed. She knew that you could never go so far that God couldn't reach you and pull you back. The real question was would Daniel want to come back to God? Had he gone so far in the other direction that he wouldn't want to return? Meghan bowed her head and prayed for Daniel. For as much as he had hurt her, they went too far back to ever give up on each other. She prayed for his love of God to return. He had once wanted to change the world for God. Now he changed, but he wasn't going to win the world for God. He was like a ship that had been dry-docked. There had to be some way to get Daniel back into the water. As soon as she said it, she knew the answer. It was the simplest thing in the world, and yet at times the hardest. She needed to pray for him.

Daniel had played a lot of sports growing up and hated it when the coach ever put him on the bench. Meg sighed. Right now, in the game of life, Daniel had put himself on the bench. The world was passing him by, and instead of being a player, he was being a spectator. It wasn't like him. Prayer again came to her mind. That was how Daniel was going to get back in the game. He needed a lot of prayer.

The public address system interrupted Meg's thoughts. Pastor Sherman was starting his sermon. Meg prayed that God would help her focus and put life's problems on hold for now.

Pastor Sherman was preaching on God's will. "You have a desire to do God's will for your life and when you start out doing it, people around you try to convince you that you're not doing God's will." Pastor Sherman laughed. "I've had people tell me that, if what you're doing is really God's will, then I support you one hundred percent; but are you really sure that it is God's will? They push, they interrogate and dig deeper than anyone has the right to. They ask me, are you totally sure it's God's will?"

He paused thoughtfully. "They go on to plant the seeds of doubt in my mind. They kindly remind me that I really don't have a lot of experience with God's will. How can I be so sure? Then they go on to tell me what I'm saying doesn't quite sound logical. You know, they look at me strangely; it doesn't really make sense."

Pastor Sherman let out a loud laugh. "If I listened to certain nay sayers around me I'd never be doing God's will. One thing that I've learned about God's will is that His ways don't always make sense to us." Pastor Sherman laughed. "You see, there's nothing wrong with His ways. What's wrong is our vision of His ways. You see, we're trying so hard to understand Heavenly concepts with our earthly understanding. We can't. We're using the wrong tools. If we want to truly understand Heavenly ways, we must look at life through our Father's eyes. He sees things differently, and His approach is often times not the same as our approach. Do you know why that is?" Meghan found herself leaning forward in anticipation.

"God doesn't want us to be able to do His will for our lives in our own power and in our own strength. God wants us to walk by faith and have no other choice but to really rely on Him to make His plans succeed."

Pastor Sherman smiled at the audience. "Do you know what happens when we follow His plan His way?" He paused for a minute. "We grow! We grow closer to God and we learn to rely on Him and He makes His will for us happen in our lives." Pastor Sherman glanced down at his notes. "Remember, a key to this entire process is that God wants to use a willing heart. No one wants to team up with a partner that's not willing. If you have a willing heart, God will fill it. He will use your life, and you will be greatly blessed for it."

At the end of the service, a bunch of the seniors wanted to go on shore to the town gazebo. Alton Bay always served coffee and donuts, and they wanted a part of it.

After Meg had docked her boat at the town dock, the seniors, with Lindy leading the pack, made their way straight for the food. She smiled. Even though they were old, they weren't so different than the kids. They knew a good deal when they saw it, and free food was always a good deal.

Someone tapped Meghan on the shoulder, and she swung around to face a smiling Reid Kensington. "What did you think of the service this morning?"

She couldn't help but smile back at him. "I thought it was really good. I want to do God's will in my life; I just sometimes get confused about what God's will is for me."

"Why is that?" Reid asked interestedly.

"Well," Meg paused reflectively, "when I start doing something that I think is God's will in my life, someone usually comes along and messes me up."

"In what way?" Reid took a step closer to her.

Meghan smiled. "I don't think it's God's will that they have a problem with. I think their problem is with me."

Reid studied her thoughtfully. "Go on," he encouraged her.

"Sometimes I feel like they doubt God's choice for His will. You know," Meghan hesitated, "it's like they're saying, why in the world would a great God use a nobody like me. There are so many people out there that are so much more qualified for the job than me." Meghan sighed. "I think people have the problem with me, not God."

Reid smiled. "If you are God's choice for a particular plan, then their problem really is with God and not you. You have to remember, He chose you, Meghan. You know," Reid put an arm around her shoulders for a second, "they may think that you are a nobody, but God knows better."

Reid withdrew his arm. "I bet David felt this way."

"David who?" Meg asked curiously.

"You know," Reid spread his arms wide, "David in the Bible."

"You're reading the Bible?" Meg couldn't contain her shock.

Reid laughed. "Yes, I told that you I became a Christian. Why does it surprise you so that I'm reading the Bible?"

Meghan shrugged. "I'm not sure…"

"There is so much in the Bible," Reid went on excitedly. "Do you know that last Wednesday I stayed up the entire night reading the Bible?"

"Really?" Meghan wished she didn't sound as surprised as she was.

Reid grinned. "I think Simon almost passed out when he found me."

"Anyway," Reid continued, "God's will. Meghan," he said honestly, "my advice to you is don't let the doubters get to you. It's just like an election. When the polls show you behind, some people act like it's all over for you. You really find out who your fair-weather friends are. Anyways, you need to push on."

Reid smiled, and it warmed Meghan's heart. "In the case of God's will versus the doubters," he sounded like the lawyer he was a training to become, "it seems to me that not only do you believe in what God's called you to do, you're forgetting a key element of the picture."

"What's that?"

"That God believes in what He's called you to do. I think that's more important than anything."

Meghan tried not to look overly impressed, but she knew that she did. "I've surprised you," Reid laughed. "I'm not the same old rake that I used to be."

"I'm starting to really see that."

Reid suddenly grew serious. "Don't ever let anyone look down on you Meghan Kane." He spoke so tenderly that Meg thought she would cry. She quickly directed her attention to the ground. Reid put a hand under her chin and slowly lifted it until their eyes met. "If anyone ever takes the time to look closely at you, they will see what I have seen all along. You are an incredibly special person. You are one in a million and once people see that, they'll never look down on you again." Reid slowly took his hand away from her chin. "They will never look down on you again," he repeated tenderly, "they will only be looking up at you." He paused and smiled shyly. "I have always looked up to you a great deal."

Meghan felt frozen. She couldn't move, laugh, cry or even breathe. She had severely underestimated Reid. He had disarmed her completely with a few sweet words and a tender touch. She closed her eyes and sighed. For the first time in her life, she knew without a doubt that she was falling for the Perfect Prince. She vowed to never become part of his fan club; yet after today she knew she was in great danger of not only joining his fan club, but also becoming the president of it.

Seventeen

$\mathcal{A}$s Meghan drove her taxi from Penny's Cove on Cedar Island, all the way down to Big Rock Island, she studied her schedule for the day. Her first stop was to pick up a group of campers from the YMCA boys' camp and bring them all the way down to Weir's Beach. From Big Rock Island to Weir's Beach would be a forty-minute trip. She was glad to have the company of Webster and Lindy. It would make the time pass quicker.

Meg smiled as she looked at her little sister. Lindy had situated herself at the front of the boat, like she always did. Today she was wearing her sea captains outfit. She had a white captain's hat on that Meghan had picked up from the Army/Navy store, and a white shirt with navy blue pants. She was scanning the horizon in front of her with her telescope. Meghan laughed softly. Lindy knew how to make the most of her time on the water taxi. There was never a dull moment with her creative little sister around.

Meghan suddenly became serious as they passed Three Tree Island. That was the place that Daniel had first gotten up the courage to kiss her. There was nothing romantic about that kiss. It was more like a hard peck on the check. She felt like Daniel had hit her in the face instead of kissing her. It had actually hurt. Meghan had to laugh at the memory of it. It was pretty funny. Meg sighed. How long would it take for her to forget Daniel? When would out-of-sight really be out-of-mind? She knew that by living on Lake Winnipesaukee, with all the memories they had shared, constantly going by places they had been together, it was going to take some serious time. She knew she needed to give herself the luxury of a little healing time, but she just wanted it over. She wanted Daniel out of her heart and life for good and she knew that wasn't going to happen soon enough.

As they got closer to Big Rock Island, they could see six Girl Scouts waiting on the YMCA dock. As Meghan pulled her boat up to the pier, Web swung around and looked at her curiously. "I thought you said that we were picking up six boys."

Meghan shrugged but didn't take her eyes off the campers. "My instructions were to pick up six boys from the YMCA boy's camp and bring them to Weir's Beach."

"Meghan!" Lindy shouted, "Those are boys dressed as Girl Scouts! They are boys wearing dresses!"

Meghan and Web's mouth dropped opened in shock. "You have got to be kidding." Webster glanced back at Meghan. "Now I've seen everything."

Webster stared at the Girl Scouts offensively. "You are not going to let them in the boat, are you?"

Before Meghan could answer, one of the Girl Scouts stepped toward her. "We have to wear these outfits as an initiation thing."

Webster stared at the boy and shook his head. "Don't you dare step on this boat yet." He turned back to Meghan. "You're not letting them on, are you. Please," he begged, "please say you're not letting them on."

Meghan exhaled loudly. She wasn't crazy about taking a forty minute ride with a bunch of boys dressed as Girl Scouts, but she also knew she didn't have much choice about it either. When her father gave her the day's schedule, he expected her to follow it. "Web," Meghan answered regretfully, "I have to pick up who my dad tells me to. I don't have a choice."

"But not them!" Web threw a hand at the offending Scouts. "I'm sure he would understand."

Meghan shook her head. "I'm sure he wouldn't. Every person is a fare and every fare keeps the marina going." She turned to the green uniformed boys. "Get on board. I want you to sit up front. Lindy," Meg ordered firmly, "get back here with me."

"I want to sit with the Girl Scouts." Lindy didn't move.

"They're not Girl Scouts," Web growled. "They're troubled individuals in need of some serious therapy."

"Lindy, get back here now." Meghan used a tone of voice that Lindy recognized as nonnegotiable. The little girl reluctantly and very unenthusiastically moved to the back of the boat to sit next to her sister.

One boy, who looked to be around fourteen, seemed to particularly enjoy Webster's discomfort. The look in his eye told Meg that Webster was about to get ranked on. "We are not Girl Scouts," the boy stated pompously, "we prefer to be called Girl Scout persons."

Web glared at the Girl Scout person. "I prefer to call you emotionally unstable, unglued, unbalanced, unhinged...just a little off your rocker," Web spread his hands wide, "and just plain nuts. That about sums it up."

"I believe I'm completely misunderstood," the boy whined dramatically. Meghan thought if he kept up his performance he might win an Oscar for it.

Web looked fiercely at the Girl Scout person. "Have you no sense of pride? God made you a man, act like a man. Be proud of it and leave the dresses for the ladies."

"I do act like a man," he protested.

"Not dressed like that you don't." Web shook his head. "Guys don't wear dresses."

"In Scotland they do." The Girl Scout person smiled proudly while he adjusted his little green hat.

"OK," Web put a hand up, "I'd like to make a few points here. First of all, some men in Scotland wear skirts. They aren't dresses and a Scotsman would probably deck a weenie like you for saying they were. They have a very manly name to their skirt. It's called a kilt. You," Web pointed a finger at the boy, "are the only man I know that wears a dress."

"It's an initiation thing."

"What's that?" Lindy asked. She hadn't taken her eyes off the boys. Meghan smiled. It wasn't every day that Lindy got to see a bunch of boys dressed up as Girl Scouts.

"An initiation is when you have to do something silly that someone else tells you to do."

"Why do you want to do that?" Lindy looked at the head Scout.

"We need to do it to pass a test."

Webster shook his head. It was clear that the boys really irritated him to no end. As he spotted the box of cookies in one of the Girl Scout person's lap, he scowled at him. "Tell me you're not going to sell them."

"We have to," the boy fiddled with his Girl Scout sash. "Is this thing even? It's so hard to keep it straight."

Web refused to acknowledge the Girl Scout person's fashion problems. "Those aren't even Girl Scout cookies," Web complained.

The head Girl Scout person shrugged. "They wouldn't give us real Girl Scout cookies."

"No wonder," Web scowled. "You're a disgrace to the uniform. You should really be ashamed of yourselves."

The boys seemed to enjoy baiting Web immensely and grinned at him as though he had given them a compliment. "We have to sell…"

Web held both hands up at the boy. "You know what, I don't want to know. I simply don't want to know. In thirty more minutes, you'll all be off my boat."

The boy ignored Web's protests. "We have to sell a box of cookies to pass the test."

Web couldn't seem to help himself. For as much as he wanted to ignore the offending scouts, they knew how to push his buttons to keep him part of the ridiculous conversation. "You have got to be kidding? Do you honestly think anyone in their right mind is going to buy Girl Scout cookies, that aren't really Girl Scout cookies, from Girl Scouts, that aren't really Girl Scouts?"

"We could pass as really ugly girls," one boy quickly pointed out.

Web groaned. "Man, there isn't a girl alive as ugly as you."

The boy pretended to be insulted. "I actually thought I looked kind of cute."

"You don't look cute," Web muttered, "you look sick. Get some help before it's too late."

The head Girl Scout person grinned at Web. "Do you think that this shade of green makes me look fat?" The boy looked down at his dress. "I know that first impressions count and I want to look my best."

Meghan tried to muffled her laugh, but Web heard it anyway and swung around to give her a dirty look. "You had better not be laughing at them. I don't want to encourage this type of behavior."

"It wasn't a laugh," Meghan smiled, "it was a burp."

Web stared at her and then looked back at the boys. "Do you do every dumb thing that someone tells you to do?"

The Girl Scout person appeared thoughtful. "Well, not every single dumb thing…" he paused. "No, you know," he waved a hand in the air, " I pretty much do every single dumb thing that I'm told to do." The boys all laughed.

"Who's idea was it for you to dress up as Girl Scouts?"

"Now I told you this before," the boy warned, "I prefer to be called a Girl Scout person."

Web glared at him. "I think I prefer not to talk to you anymore. Stay on that side of the boat. Don't talk to me, and don't let me catch you looking at me."

The boy crossed his arms in a huff. "You're not even my type."

"Be quiet," Web threatened, "or I may have to hurt you."

"Does this mean that you're not going to buy any of my cookies?"

"I'm turning around," Web mumbled, "and I'm pretending that you're not here."

When the boys couldn't get any more reactions out of Webster, they entertained themselves by waving at passing boaters. Meghan had to laugh at the expression of disbelief on the boaters faces as they passed. It wasn't every day that you saw a boy dressed as a Girl Scout waving at you. It would make interesting dinner conversation.

Meghan was thankful that she had never been forced to do some stupid prank. Every summer some of the camps put their campers though ridiculous initiations. The boys camps were always worse than the girls camps. Meghan smiled as she remember the boy's camp that had a group of boys dress up in girls clothes, complete with wigs and then water ski around the lake. That was a scene she knew she would never forget.

As they docked at Weir's Beach, people were already starting to stare at the strange looking scouts. Web took his sunglasses and baseball cap out of his knapsack and tried to disguise himself. He had made it clear that he wanted no part of this

He turned to Meghan and slid his sunglasses down a bit. "We're not picking them up, are we?"

"I have to, Web," Meghan shrugged. "My dad had it on the schedule."

"Then do me a favor," he pulled the brim of his hat lower, "drop me off at home before you pick them up. I don't think I can take another ride with them. I don't want to hear their stories, and I don't want to know if they've sold their cookies."

Meghan smiled sympathetically at her friend. "No problem, Web."

"Promise me that you won't bring this Girl Scout person thing up again."

Meghan laughed. "Not to you."

Web nodded. "OK, I can live with that." He glanced at the boys walking down the boardwalk. "I just don't get it. Why would anyone do that?" He looked at Meghan for an explanation. "I'd have to be dead for anyone to do that to me. That's so embarrassing."

"They don't seem to think so."

"They have a problem."

Meghan laughed. "I think you may be right."

"I know I'm right." Web shook his head. He was almost as funny as the boys.

Eighteen

$\mathcal{F}$riday night the gang met at Little Beach to play football. A bonfire was already crackling by the time that Meghan pulled her boat upon the beach. She could see three sets of car headlights illuminating the beach. Playing football at night was always a summer favorite.

At one end of the beach, she could hear Simon and Web arguing about who was going to be quarterback. "You can't be quarterback," Web stated matter of factly.

"Why not?" Simon demanded.

"Well, for starters, you can't throw."

"I could hit you anywhere on this beach."

Web laughed. "Man, you couldn't even hit the lake if you fell into it."

Meghan's eyes caught someone coming toward her from the other end of the beach. As she identified Daniel's tall, lanky figure, her stomach instantly knotted. She had no idea that he would be here.

"Hey," he said easily.

"Hey, yourself."

"Can I speak with you for a minute?"

Meghan knew she really didn't have much of a choice. "Make it quick."

"I love you."

Meghan stared at him for a second, not sure she had heard him right. As she looked at him closer, she knew by the expression on his face that she had. "That was quick," she whispered.

"Meghan, I'm real sorry about everything." Daniel shoved his hands deep into his jeans pockets. "I'm not sure how we ever got to this point."

"You dumped me for Brittany," Meghan responded flatly.

"I think that the whole idea of forever just scared me. We'd never dated anyone else but each other."

"I never asked you to give me an engagement ring." Meghan was disgusted. If he thought he could pin this on her, he was very wrong.

"Yeah, but you expected it."

"Not now I didn't. Not while we were still in high school."

"Why did you accept my ring if you didn't want to get engaged?"

"Why did you give me a ring if you didn't want to get engaged?"

Daniel sighed. "I didn't want to lose you."

Meghan felt her fist clench at her sides. "Oh yeah, I believe we had this little discussion. You wanted to get engaged so you wouldn't lose me, but you also wanted to date other girls. That's not the way it works, Daniel. When two people become engaged, they're supposed to commit to each other. You can't have it both ways."

"I just needed time."

"I never pressured you. Now I see it clearly. It's amazing what a little hindsight can do for a situation. You wanted to make sure that I didn't date anyone and would hang around for you while you went and dated Brittany. Did you think I was so stupid that I'd actually go along with that plan?"

"I'm sorry, Meghan. I really never planned on dating Brittany."

"You're worse than sorry. You're pathetic."

"I still think that we are meant to be together forever."

"Now you're delusional."

"Meg, I just got a little sidetracked."

Meghan sighed. "Brittany was a major detour."

"She was a mistake."

"What exactly are you saying, Daniel?"

"I want you back." The word came out in an airy rush.

"Have you broken up with Brittany?"

"I will."

"So," Meghan said sarcastically, "you're keeping Brittany on the back burner just in case I say no."

"It's not like that."

"It's exactly like that. You're not being fair to either one of us, Daniel. If you really loved me, you wouldn't come to me with Brittany still in your pocket. You're insulting."

"You're right. I'm sorry."

"You need to get one thing straight. I will never, ever come back to you." Meghan didn't realize the truth of that statement until she verbalized it.

"Is it because of Reid?" Daniel asked accusingly.

"No, Daniel," Meghan shook her head, "it's because of you. I don't trust you anymore. I don't love you."

"Do you love Reid?"

Meghan eyed him hard. "That's not a question that you get to ask anymore."

"Don't marry him unless you love him, Meg."

"Are you still trying to tell me what to do?"

"I could never tell you what to do." Daniel scuffed the sand with his toe. "Don't marry him, Meg."

Meghan sighed frustrated. 'We're not even dating."

"You will be."

"You think you know me so well."

Daniel laughed nervously. "I do know you so well. We've been together practically all of our lives."

"If you know me so well, you wouldn't have dumped me for Brittany and then thought you could get me back."

"I made a big mistake. Can't we ever get beyond that?"

"You're still dating Brittany and you ask me that? You have got to be kidding!"

"We go back such a long way," Daniel pleaded. "We have so much history together."

Meghan felt the sting of tears coming on. "Daniel, we have been trapped in the past for so long. It's time we got over it and moved on. We need to move on if we're ever going to have hope or a future."

"A future together?" Daniel asked hopefully.

"No," Meghan answered sadly. "We will never have a future together. Get on with your life, Daniel, and let me get on with mine."

As Meghan walked away from him, she didn't look back. As she heard him start his motorboat engine, she didn't look back. For once in her life, she knew she had to move on; and to do that, she knew it meant never looking back.

Reid showed up ten minutes after Daniel had left. He found Meghan quietly standing by the bonfire. "Why are you all by yourself?"

"I guess I'm just not very social tonight."

"Is there a reason for that?"

"Daniel." The one word answer said it all.

"Was he here tonight?"

"He just left."

"He upset you?"

"Yes, but not for the reasons you think."

"What reasons then?"

"He thinks he can dump me and get me back whenever he wants."

"He broke up with Brit?" Reid asked, stepping so close to Meghan that there hands were almost touching.

"No," Meghan laughed nervously. "I think he was checking out his options."

"Are you an option?"

"He thought so."

"Are you?" Reid repeated patiently.

"Not for him."

"How about for me?" Reid sounded so vulnerable it touched Meg's heart.

"Maybe," she answered cautiously.

"You know I have a past, Meghan. Please don't judge me by it. I'm changing with God's help."

Meghan nodded. "I can't commit to anything right now. I feel so messed up inside."

Reid smiled kindly. "How about friendship? Can you commit to friendship?"

Meghan smiled. "Yes, I can do that."

Reid stuck his hand out and Meghan shook it. As soon as their hands touched, Meg felt a slight tremor run through her body. As she looked into Reid's smoldering eyes, she knew he had felt it too.

"I can only be friends," Meghan whispered weakly.

Reid nodded. "I'll never push you, Meg. I won't ever take what you don't offer."

He squeezed her hand and let go of it. "Can I ask you something?"

Meghan laughed. "Why do I get the feeling that it's going to be personal?"

Reid's blue eyes lit with humor. "Probably because it is."

"That's the worst kind of question."

"There's something that I need to know."

Meghan braced herself. "Do you still love Daniel?"

Meghan felt herself relax. "Not anymore."

"You were together a long time."

"Dumping me for Brittany and then trying to get back with me while he was still dating Brittany helped me get over him fast."

"Are you sure?" The question hung in Reid's eyes and Meg knew it had to be settled.

"As sure as I can be."

"I don't ever want you dating me and wishing I were Daniel."

Meghan gasped. "I would never ever do that."

"Good." Reid took Meghan's hand and playfully laced their fingers together. "So, do you want to go to a movie this weekend?"

"As friends?" Meghan slanted a look at him.

"If that's the way it's got to be."

Meghan nodded. "That's the way it's got to be."

"For now?" Reid hoped for a future that promised something different.

"For now," Meg admitted and smiled. "You know, I actually think that I'm starting to like you."

Reid grinned. "That's a good start. You've helped me to change, Meg."

"God helped you to change, Reid." Meg smiled. "I just kicked you in the right direction. You are such a special person. God has put you in a unique position to change the world for Him!" Meghan laughed. "Don't blow it!"

Reid joined her laughter. "That's another thing that I like about you. You don't beat around the bush. You come right out and say exactly what it is that you're thinking."

"Life is too short to play games. Beating around the bush is a waste of time."

"Don't ever change, Meg. That's an admirable quality."

"Thanks."

"Thanks for believing in me. You don't know what a wonderful gift that is for me."

"Reid, if you follow God, I know He's going to lead you to do great things in your life."

"I think that you have more confidence about God working in my life than I do." A troubled expression crossed his face. "My past was very selfish."

Meghan took his hand and squeezed it tightly. "You're past is in the past. It has been washed cleaned by the blood of Jesus. God sees you as clean now."

"That really amazes me."

"Don't you think that God could have bigger plans for your life than you do or your father does?"

Reid smiled. "My father's plans are pretty grand."

"So are your Heavenly Father's!"

"Don't tell dad that right now. I'm not sure he could handle it."

"Reid," Meghan said earnestly, "don't let anyone sell yourself short and that includes you, too."

"That's easier said than done."

"I didn't say it was easy." Meg smiled gently. "God's plans are always better then what any person could ever try to arrange or put together. Don't limit yourself. If you follow God and His plans for your life, He will show you what you're supposed to do."

"Sometimes I think I get stuck on only what I see right before me." As Reid paused, Meghan could see his struggle. "I'm not the most patient of men. This faith thing is going to take some time."

"Reid," Meghan's voice was sympathetic, "you've only just become a Christian. As you grow closer to God, it gets easier to take things on faith."

Reid laughed. "I'll have to take your word on that."

"Don't try to figure out the entire Christian life overnight. Let God lead you one step at a time."

"I think that's good advice. I tend to look down the road too far and try to figure everything out."

"God has given you wonderful gifts. He gave you the ability to speak before people with ease and sincerity. You're a people person and people are drawn to you." Meg paused. "Think of all the good that you can do. Did it ever occur to you that God has given you these gifts to serve Him?"

"No," his face scrunched up, "I hadn't thought of things that way before."

"Well, you better," Meghan smiled. "Our gifts are given to us that we might bring glory to God."

Reid grinned. "I have a lot to learn."

"You will," Meghan added quickly.

"Thanks, Meghan," Reid's voice sounded choked up. "Thanks for being there for me and believing in me."

"Reid, I do believe in you and what God is doing in your life."

"My past haunts me at times." Reid shook his head sadly. "I have so many things that I regret."

"Don't limit your future by living in your past. You're a child of the King now. Let Him rule your life."

"I plan to, Meghan. I want my future to be so different than my past. I've messed my life up by trying to run it. I'm more than happy to let God take the reins."

"You can't even imagine what God can do with a person that is fully committed to Him."

"I'm hoping I'll find out." Reid's eyes were brimming with tears.

"You will," Meghan smiled gently. "I know you will."

Nineteen

As Meghan drove her water taxi full of seniors toward the docks at Weir's Beach, she could see one lone person standing in the Cedar Island Taxi pick-up point. Meghan watched the person curiously. She didn't have any scheduled pick-ups.

As her boat grew closer to the dock, she could see the customer was a woman. She looked to be middle age, with long brown hair halfway down her back. Meghan's attention was drawn to a cigarette that dangled from the front of her mouth. Something about this lady seemed strangely familiar. She had an impatience about her that Meg could spot from a distance. She was in constant motion, pacing the docks back and forth, fiddling agitatedly with a brown, long necked beer bottle.

Meghan shook her head. Even the cigarette that dangled from the front of her mouth seemed familiar. Her mother used to smoke like that all the time. The cigarette wasn't at either side of her mouth in was always right in the middle dangling. Her mother.... Meghan gasped so loudly that the Hobson's turned and stared at her.

"Are you all right?" Roy asked her in a concerned voice.

Meghan simply nodded at the older man. She couldn't have found words at that moment if her life had depended on it. She felt almost paralyzed with shock. Her mother, who was absolutely her worst nightmare, had returned to Lake Winnipesaukee. It was neither a heart-warming sight nor a welcoming one.

The worst years of her life had been when her mother was around. She was drunk and nasty most of the time. She lived in an old faded orange bathrobe and always had a cigarette hanging from her lips. Meghan cringed. To this day she hated the color orange because of its association with her mother.

Her childhood had been far from ideal. When she watched TV and saw happy families, she inwardly questioned if anyone could have such a life. It seemed too perfect and too much to hope for to have a mom and a dad that loved each other and their kids. She had neither.

Her mom would verbally assault her and beat her for no reason at all. Meghan had always tried to be good for her mom. She cleaned the house, took care of Lindy, and tried to stay quiet to keep her happy. She stayed quieter than any kid should have, but it was more out of fear than respect.

As Meghan watched her mother on the docks, the harsh memories continued to assault her and overwhelm her. She shook her head. How strange was it that she lived with her mother for eleven years, and she couldn't even think of one single positive memory. All she had was bad memories and a lifetime of nightmares.

As Meghan continued to watch her mother, her heart began to harden and she became very determined not to live through the nightmares again. She had barely survived the first time. She knew that the second time she might not be as fortunate. She vowed, then and there, not to willing put herself or Lindy under her mother's evil ways again.

Meghan instantly changed course. Instead of steering the boat toward the west dock, which was her usual pick up point, she steered her boat toward the east dock on the other side of Weir's Beach.

Her passengers turned and looked at her with questioning eyes. "We're docking at the east side today." Meghan knew she could never explain the situation. She was still so ashamed of her mother. "I'll pick you up at the west side dock at three."

Meghan tapped Miss Birdie on the shoulder. "Can you please take Lindy with you today?"

"Certainly, dear," Miss Birdie quickly agreed. "What's wrong?"

Meghan didn't say anything; she simply glanced back at the west dock. Miss Birdie followed the girl's eyes, and soon her face darkened. "Is that her?" Miss Birdie asked pointedly.

Meghan nodded. "Yes." She answered in a quiet, pained whisper.

"I wonder why she's come back?" Miss Birdie asked thoughtfully. "She must want something."

"Probably money," Meghan said disgustedly. "The other times she's come back in the past it has always been for money."

"You don't have any money," Miss Birdie protested. "The marina runs on a shoestring budget as it is. She knows that."

"She's never cared. She'd bleed us dry if she could."

"Meg," Miss Birdie whispered hopefully, "maybe she's changed."

Meghan slowly shook her head. "I doubt it. She still has her cigarette in one hand and her beer in the other. Who drinks beer at nine in the morning?"

"Someone addicted to it," Miss Birdie solemnly admitted.

Meghan nodded. "I don't want Lindy to know that she's here. She'll be brokenhearted when she leaves again."

"How do you plan to hide her from Lindy and your father?"

"I'm docking on the east side to give you time to get Lindy off the boardwalk before my mother makes it over here. I don't want Lindy seeing her. She only puts us down and tramples us both."

"It's probably due to a lot of guilt."

"I don't care what it's from. I'm tired of getting steamrolled by her." Meghan sighed. "She was never a mother to us Birdie, you were. Just because that woman on the docks gave birth to Lindy and I doesn't make her a mother. It was clear from the start that she never wanted the job."

"That was no reflection on you girls," Miss Birdie squeezed Meghan's hand. "She was always too selfish a person to care about anyone but herself."

"She should have never had kids." Meghan was fighting back the angry tears that were threatening to spill down her cheeks.

"I'm glad she did, Sweetie," Miss Birdie said gently. "I don't know what I'd ever do without you and Lindy."

Meghan managed a slight smile at the kind old woman that had taken care of them. "Please see that you keep Lindy away from her?"

"Yes, dear, of course I will. I told Lindy that I would take her school shopping. What I didn't tell her," Miss Birdie smiled, "was that I was going to take her shopping today. I'm sure we'll have a wonderful time."

Meghan nodded and smiled. Her little sister was a clotheshorse. "I'm sure she'll love it. Thanks, Birdie. I love you."

"I love you, too, dear," Miss Birdie glanced back at the west dock again. "Your mother must have figured out that you're not docking there. She's making her way to the east docks."

Meghan saw her and nodded. "She doesn't seem to be in any kind of a hurry. You'll have plenty of time to get Lindy into town."

"How are you going to keep your father from finding out about her?"

"Well," Meghan paused thoughtfully, "I figure that if I don't taxi her out to Cedar Island, she can't get there. Dad will never find out."

"That's a good plan. You are the only taxi that goes all the way to the southern islands. She could never afford to hire a private charter. The less your father finds out, the better off things will be. She always sends him into a drunken depression."

"I've been thinking about my options for a while just in case she ever returned." Meg sighed. "I always hoped she wouldn't, but somehow I knew that she would."

After Meghan's passengers disembarked, she bought herself a little more time and drove her boat back to the east dock. She got out on the boardwalk and waited for the inevitable unpleasant reunion.

"What do you think that you're doing docking on the east side instead of the west side?"

Meghan bit her lip. It was the greeting that she was expecting but not the one that the little girl inside her was hoping for. She sighed. She knew in her heart that a part of her would always long to hear loving words from a mother that would never give them.

As she narrowed her eyes, studying the calloused woman before her, she knew for that reason alone she needed to keep Lindy away from her. Meghan had suffered enough for both of them. She didn't want her bright, sensitive, imaginative sister to go through the pain that she had. Once was more than enough for both of them. She would protect Lindy at all costs.

"Did you hear me?" A hard, cold voice demanded.

"Yes," Meghan answered quietly. "The passengers had to get off at the east dock today."

"Why?" Her mother was looking at her carefully.

"They had appointments in that part of town." What she couldn't say was that she had let them off there to make sure she and Lindy didn't meet. That couldn't ever happen.

"I need to get to Cedar Island," her mother oozed with impatience.

Meghan stared at her mother and knew that her plan was going to be harder to implement than she had originally thought. Fear shivered down her spine, and Meg prayed for God to help her. Standing up to her mother was something that she had never done before.

"I need to go now." Her mother's irritation was heating up her legendary temper.

Instinctively Meghan took a step backwards. Once again she prayed for strength. "No," the word was no louder than a whisper but carried with it all the conviction that Meg felt. "I won't bring you."

"What did you say?" Her mother's cigarette twitched angry in her mouth.

Meghan sighed. Why did people always ask you what you said when they knew perfectly well what you said. Meg knew that repeating her answer wouldn't make her mother like it any better. "I said no."

Her mother took an aggressive step toward her, and Meghan flinched as she saw her hand rise in the air. It was an action she was all too familiar with. It was always how the physical abuse started. First her mother would raise her voice, and then she'd raise her hand. After that, the abuse would snowball.

Meghan automatically braced herself. She was surprised to see her mother's hand stop halfway to her face. A second later, she saw the reason why. Local Sheriff, Jimmy Stewart was standing just off to the side of them. Meghan watched her mother staring at him.

"What seems to be the problem here?" Jimmy glanced at her mother and then directed his full attention to Meghan.

As Meghan looked at Jimmy, she knew that God had just answered her prayer. She was never more thankful to see the strong arm of the law in all her life. Jimmy Stewart was a quiet but powerful presence around the lake. It wasn't his physical appearance that had people quaking in their shoes. He looked like Barney Fife but acted more like Arnold Schwarzenegger. He took his oath to uphold the law very seriously. He had the strength of steel inside him that almost begged anyone to challenge his authority. He wore the badge, and he knew how to use it. It was an unfortunate person that underestimated his strength and ability.

"Meghan?" Jimmy asked questioningly. "Is there anything that you want to tell me?"

Meghan nodded slowly. "She was going to hit me." Meghan was not sure where the words had come from or the courage to actually say them out loud. Once again she knew that God was with her.

Jimmy took a step towards Meghan's mother. He didn't have a clue as to who she was because Jimmy had come to the lake long after Meg's mother had left. "Do you realize that's assault?" He leaned in close to her mother. "You can't go around just hitting people."

"I didn't hit her," her mother responded defiantly.

"You would have if I hadn't been here." Jimmy's voice was threateningly calm.

"She's my daughter. I can hit her if I want to."

Meghan's mother had chosen to challenge the wrong lawman. Jimmy's eyes narrowed angrily. "I'd like to see some identification—now." Her mother rummaged through her pocketbook before producing a license that claimed her to be Celia Kane.

"Your license has expired." Jimmy stared from the license picture to her mother's face.

"I'm not driving with it. You asked for an ID and I gave you an ID."

Jimmy stared at Celia for a full minute before speaking. "Has anyone ever told you that it's very unwise to irritate someone with a badge?"

"I don't kiss up to anyone!" The anger in Celia's voice made Meghan shudder. Anyone with half a brain knew that you didn't push Jimmy Stewart around.

Jimmy's face took on a cold hard look. "Meghan is this really your mother?"

"Yes, Sir, "Meghan admitted regretfully. It wasn't something that she had ever been proud of.

"Do you want to press charges against her?"

"What in the world?" Celia took the cigarette out of her mouth and pointed it at Jimmy like a sword. "Are you trying to turn my own kid against me?"

She dropped her half smoked cigarette on the dock and crushed it out with her foot.

"I imagine you turned your kids against you all by yourself, Mrs. Kane." Jimmy leveled her with a chilling look. "You don't exactly strike me as the mother of the year type." Jimmy turned to Meghan and his face softened. "Do you want to press charges against her? You have the right to."

"How dare you!" Celia's temper got the best of her.

"Quiet or I'll take you away right now." Jimmy watched her long enough to make sure she would stay quiet.

"Meghan?" Jimmy questioned. "This is your call."

"I don't understand," Meghan looked confused.

"I could write her up now for attempted battery and assault. Just because she didn't hit you doesn't mean that she wasn't going to. I was here. I witnessed the whole thing."

Celia opened her mouth to speak, and Jimmy pointed a hand in her direction. "Don't make me have to talk to you again. Understand?" Celia didn't nod, but Meg was sure she had understood.

"Meghan," Jimmy's voice became gentle, "no one ever has the right to hit you," Jimmy glanced at Celia, "not even your own mother." He paused. "Has it happened before?"

Meghan couldn't answer. She was all choked up and felt like she was going to cry. No one had ever helped her stand up to her mother before. Never in all her life did she suspect that Jimmy Stewart was going to be her Knight in Shining Armor to save her from her own mother.

"Meghan," Jimmy lay a comforting hand on her shoulder, "let me help you through this. That's what I'm here for."

Meghan slowly nodded. She knew she did need help. If her mother somehow made it to Cedar Island, she would disrupt the lives of everyone she came in contact with for a long time. She was like the nightmare that kept on living.

Meghan turned and looked at her mother. "If you leave now, I won't press charges against you."

"Why you…" Celia looked completely outraged.

Jimmy cut her off. "Quiet. You will only answer when you are spoken to and you will answer respectfully." Jimmy stared at her at moment before continuing. "Meghan's offer was for you to leave and she wouldn't press any charges." Jimmy paused and Meghan saw the rage return to his eyes. "I personally think that she should nail you with whatever she can." Jimmy sighed. "But this decision is hers. Do you accept the offer?"

"So it's come down to this?" Celia muttered at her daughter.

"Yes," Meghan found strength in her conviction. "It's come down to the fact that I promise to defend myself, Lindy and Dad. If you threaten us in any way, I'll make sure the Sheriff knows about it." Meghan paused as she watched shock mixed with anger cover her mother's face.

"After all I've done for you," Celia snarled. "This is what I get for everything I did for you?"

Meghan's anger began to boil over. "After all you've done for me? For me?" Meg pointed a finger at her. "Isn't it more like after everything you did to me. You abused for me years." Meghan eyed her mother with contempt. "After everything you did to me you should be in jail." Meghan clenched her fists at her side. "Go away now or I'll have you arrested."

Sheriff Stewart, who had placed himself between the two of them, slowly turned his head back and forth. As he turned back to Celia, he ordered in a cold tone, "Make your choice now. Time's up."

Celia took one last livid look at Meghan and slowly turned to go. Meghan watched her make her way from the boardwalk to the street. She wasn't sure how her mother had gotten to Lake Winnipesaukee and she wasn't sure how she was going to leave. All that mattered right now was that she left. Meg bit back more tears. Even though her mother was going away, she doubted that the physical and emotional scars she had caused would ever go away. A lifetime would not be enough time to erase them.

"Meghan," Jimmy asked softly, "are you going to be OK?"

All Meghan could do was nod her head. The emotional pain was strangling her. After all these years the pain was still so raw and so deep.

"What you did back there was very brave."

"Or incredibly stupid. She may come back later."

"If she does, you will call me and I'll take care of her." Jimmy looked directly into her tear filled brown eyes. "I know that I may look rather wimpy but I know how to use my badge and gun. I enforce the law Meghan. Call me 24/7 and let me do my job."

Meghan nodded. She was still trying to come to grips with the fact that Jimmy was offering to help defend her against the meanest monster in her life. No one ever had before.

"Has this happened before?"

Shame covered Meghan's face. "Yes," she whispered.

"Meghan, you have nothing to be ashamed of. She should be ashamed. You are the victim here, and I'm going to help you." Jimmy's eyes took on urgency. "Please, let me help you through this. That's what I'm here for."

Once again, all Meghan could do was nod. She felt so totally overwhelmed.

"I've watched you since I moved up here to the lake. You always had so much responsibility between running the taxi and taking care of Lindy."

"I don't regret any of it."

Jimmy smiled warmly. "I didn't say that you did. I'm just hoping that you're going to take some time to be a kid while you're still technically a kid."

Meghan's mouth dropped open, and Jimmy laughed. "I'm a good lawman Meghan. I notice what goes on around me. I notice all the things that people never tell me. What someone does is a lot more important than what they say."

"That's true."

"You should be proud of yourself. You are the glue that keeps your family together. Now," Jimmy sighed frustrated, "let me be the enforcer that keeps your mother from hurting you any further."

Meghan nodded. "Thank you." The voice was weak but it was filled with a sincerity and relief that Sheriff Stewart did not miss.

As Sheriff Stewart turned to go, he paused. "Remember, I am here for you 24/7."

"I will."

"Good," he winked at her, "because if you forget it Meghan Kane, I will gladly remind you of it."

Meghan glanced at her watch and found that she had almost two hours before she had to taxi her seniors home. She sighed. That would be plenty of time to get to Bug Lighthouse. She needed a secluded spot to cry and then be able to get herself together before she had to face Lindy again. The little girl was too perceptive and would instantly know that something was wrong.

As she docked at the little lighthouse, she quickly made her way down a pine-covered path through the woods. There was a huge fallen log, about halfway through the woods that she crawled up on like a small child. The pine trees that surrounded her acted as a shield against the outside world. It was the perfect place to go when you needed a little privacy. She could be herself there and open up and bawl her eyes out if that's what she needed to do.

That's exactly what Reid found her doing ten minutes later. She was sitting on the log with her head in her hands crying her heart out like it had been broken into a million pieces. Alarm slammed through him as he saw her. Whatever had happened to make his normally calm and collected friend fall apart was something that he intended to avenge right away.

He gathered her up in his arms and held her gently like he would a broken doll. He didn't ask her questions. Now was the time to comfort her. Later he would question her and then seek justice against whoever had done this to her. He had no doubt in his mind that they would pay. For now, he fought against his impatient urge to plow ahead. He knew he needed to be patient; but right at the moment, he felt anything but patient. As he looked down into Meghan's tearful face he felt his anger burn within him. He prayed and asked God for wisdom and patience. He knew Meghan well enough to know that she would tell him in her own time. He just hoped that wasn't too long.

"My mother came to visit," Meghan choked the words out like she had a noose around her neck.

Reid sat for a moment in stunned silence. "Your mother?" He leaned over to look in her tearful eyes. "I thought your mother was dead."

Meghan shook her head slightly. "No, she's very much alive." She exhaled loudly. "She has a lot of problems."

"Problems?" Reid had been thrown for a loop. He couldn't understand how he could have known Meghan for so long and not known about her mother.

"Not many people on the lake knew what my mother was like. My family kept things quiet mainly out of shame."

"What shame could you have that you'd need to hide?"

"My mother," Meghan whispered. "She was an alcoholic and a drug user. She was nearly always drunk with a cigarette dangling from her lips."

"I never knew."

"Not many people did. It's not the type of thing you advertise, ya know?" Reid nodded sympathetically. "Every family has it's problems."

"If you're really going to be my friend, my mother is something that you're going to need to hear about. I'm not sure if I'm a person you want linked to you in a political sense."

"That is not important to me. When I said that I wanted to be your friend, I wasn't offering you a friendship with strings and stipulations."

"Thanks," Meghan felt relieved. "Are you ready to hear her story?"

"I'm ready to hear anything that you're ready to tell me."

Meghan nodded slightly. "My mom was an awful wife and mother. She cheated on my dad so much that I heard him tell Aunt Birdie that he wasn't even sure Lindy and I were his kids."

Reid's face was covered in sympathy. "Both of you look like your father."

Meghan shook her head sadly. "No, we don't. Our brown eyes and brown hair come from my mother's side."

"It doesn't prove anything."

"You're right. It doesn't prove that we're not his kids; then again, it doesn't prove that we are. I've driven myself crazy over the years trying to find any similarities between my dad and me. I'd watch the way he did things. I became acutely aware of the foods he liked, the books he liked or the movies he watched." Meg sighed and shook her head. "I just wanted so badly for something to hang onto to prove I was his."

"I'm so sorry, Meg. I really am." He pulled her close again as if it would protect her from the trouble of the world. He felt an intense need to guard, protect, and care for Meghan. She had seen too much pain in her time. He would try to make her future so much brighter.

"There's more."

A troubled sigh escaped Reid's lips. "I was afraid you'd say that."

"My mother verbally and physically abused me."

Reid's grip around Meghan tightly protectively. "I think I want to kill her."

"You'd have to stand in line. Sheriff Stewart was ready to throw her in jail this morning."

"Jimmy?"

"Yes."

"Why?"

"She almost hit me again. If he hadn't come along just at the right time she would have."

Reid was battling emotions that he never knew he had. He never knew he could feel so much anger toward another individual. His emotions bordered on pure rage. "Remind me to thank Jimmy next time I see him."

"Reid," Meghan's voice was filled with hesitancy, "if we're going to have a relationship, even if we're just friends, you're going to have to realize I come with some serious baggage."

Reid smiled tenderly. "Sweetheart, we all do. My family is living proof just how much money can mess you up."

"I guess mine is living proof of how much alcohol can mess you up. When my mother got drunk, one of her favorite pastimes was to burn her cigarettes into me."

"No," Reid sounded as if someone had slugged him.

"She was very clever about it. She would burn me in areas that others wouldn't easily see. Her favorite spots were under my arms and on my rear end."

Meghan pulled her short sleeve shirt down under the arms just enough for Reid to see horrible, thick scars. He laid his head against Meghan's chest and began to sob. He was so broken up that anyone would hurt Meg. He had always known she was very special, but now he knew something more. He loved her with all his heart, and he wanted to make sure that something like this never happened again.

"Honey," Reid's words were thick with pain, "I am so sorry for what you had to go through. I wish I had known. I wish I could have prevented it."

Meghan slipped her hand into his. "My mother used another trick on me. She told me that if I ever told anyone about this, Social Services would come and take Lindy and me away. She said that Lindy and I would be separated forever."

"That's not true."

"A little kid doesn't know that. My mother always said things so convincingly." Meghan paused. "I really thought I'd never see Lindy again; or worse, Social Services would come take me away and leave Lindy at the mercy of my mother. I didn't want Lindy to ever go through what I had gone through."

Meghan exhaled loudly, willing herself to go on. "When my mom got drunk, I would hide Lindy in the boathouse. She was a good baby. She didn't make very much noise. It's almost as if she could sense that my mother was bad and that I was protecting her."

Reid kept an arm around Meghan. "I am so sorry. I feel like I'm wearing those words out. Thank you for trusting me enough to share this with me." Reid kissed Meghan on the forehead gently. "I'm a good listener. Open up to me anytime. I have broad shoulders, and I can take it."

"Thank you," Meghan whispered sincerely.

"My second offer is one that I hope you will take up." Meghan eyed him curiously. "I want you to go see Dr. Mary Martin. She's the best psychologist that I know."

"Reid," Meghan immediately protested, "I can't afford counseling. I can barely afford to put food on the table."

"Meghan," he smiled lovingly, "I didn't intend for you to pay for it. I'm going to pay for your counseling. It's something that I can do for you."

Meghan stood up awkwardly. "Oh, no way. You're not paying for me."

Reid laughed. "I know you're used to taking care of yourself. You're going to have to swallow your pride. My family has more money than they know what to do with." He pulled her down beside him on the log again. "Listen, I couldn't help you before, because I didn't know about it. Now that I do, please let me help you. I really want to do this."

"Why?" Meghan eyed him closely. "You're doing so much more than anyone's ever done. Why do you feel the need to pay for my counseling as well?"

Reid gently took Meghan's face in his hands and tenderly smiled at her. "Why?" He echoed her words and she nodded. "Meghan, I fell for you a long time ago. I need to help you, because I love you. It's that simple for me. When someone I love is in trouble, I need to step in and help them. Please," he urged, "let me do this for you."

Meghan nodded. She was too shocked to say anything for a minute. The great Reid Kensington loved her. It boggled her mind; but as she looked into his eyes, she knew it was true. He loved her. She smiled for the first time in hours. What she also knew was true, that she hadn't been able to admit yet, was that she loved him right back. Meghan smiled again. Who would have guessed that the Perfect Prince would fall for the poor girl on the lake? They came together from opposite ends of the lake and opposites ends of life. He was filthy rich, and she was pathetically poor. He was in the popular crowd, and she was not. He hadn't had to work a day in his life and she had pretty much had to work every day in her life.

Somehow, while cradled lovingly in Reid's arms, the differences didn't seem to matter so much. They loved the Lord and loved each other and right at that moment, that was enough. That was all that mattered. That was all Meghan could see.

Twenty

The arrival of Labor Day at Lake Winnipesaukee signaled the official close of summer. The summer folks returned to their winter homes and the majority of Meghan's taxi route flew south to Florida for the colder months. It was always sad to see the islanders leave but Meghan kept in touch with many of her senior friends through letters and emails.

The lake took on a different atmosphere during the off-season. With most of the islanders gone, the major ferries stopped running, the camps closed up and life in general slowed down to a more leisurely pace.

Meghan didn't mind the solitude; in fact, she welcomed the break from her busy summer schedule. There were still plenty of people around the lake; and in the fall tourists flocked to the area to experience the beautiful foliage colors first hand. In the wintertime, the area was overrun with skiers from all over New England. Meg had to admit there really wasn't a dull season. In the spring, the cycle would start up all over again as the islanders slowly returned.

Meghan looked curiously at the pouting little girl in front of her. "I don't see why my egg route has to stop."

Meghan looked at her sister compassionately. This was the first year that Lindy had run the egg route, and it had turned out to be a huge success. Their supply couldn't keep up with their demand. For next year, they were actually thinking of expanding their route and buying more chickens.

"Lindy," Meg knelt down in front of the disgruntled little businesswoman, "I had to give up my newspaper route too. We can't sell newspapers and fresh eggs to islanders if they're not there. When spring comes, we'll start everything up again."

Lindy stared at her older sister thoughtfully. "Well, what are we going to do with all the eggs my chickens make?" Snacks head popped up and she stared at Lindy expectantly. Anytime food was being discussed, the old, overweigh dog had a hopefulness that glowed in her eyes. "I don't want to be eating eggs all winter."

Meghan nodded. "That's a good point. Neither do I."

"So what are we going to do?" Lindy stared at her sister expecting an instant answer.

Meghan laughed. "What you really mean is, what am I going to do!" Lindy nodded.

"You know," Meghan snapped her fingers together, "I bet we could sell the eggs to some of the restaurants around the lake. The bigger places stay open all year long."

"Do you think they'd buy them?" Lindy scrunched her little nose up at Meghan. "I don't want to give them away. Mr. Hobson says that giving eggs away would be bad for business."

Meghan smiled. Over the course of the summer the Hobson brothers had given Lindy all kinds of free business advice. The little five-year-old tyrant could now spout all kinds of impressive business jargon at people. Lindy was always ready to take on the world.

"Yes," Meghan laughed, "they'll pay for them. Let's start at Mountainview Restaurant. They serve three meals a day."

"Do you think they use eggs?" Lindy asked seriously.

"I'm sure they do," Meghan put an arm around her sister.

"What about brown eggs?"

Meghan laughed again. "Brown eggs are just as good as white eggs. I'm sure it will be fine."

"They're not as pretty," Lindy stated matter of fact.

"Restaurants don't buy eggs because they're pretty. They buy eggs to cook with so their customers can eat all kinds of yummy foods."

"Eggs do go into a lot of food. Miss Birdie told me that."

"Yes they do. Now let's head over to Mountainview and see if we can sell some eggs."

"I need to get at least $1.10 a dozen. If I go lower than that Mr. Hobson says I'll be eating my shirt."

Meghan laughed. "Well, we don't want that, do we?"

"No, we don't," Lindy replied seriously.

Mountainview Restaurant was so excited about buying fresh eggs throughout the wintertime, they agreed to buy Lindy out. They ordered ten dozen eggs a week, and that was the max that Lindy's chickens laid.

After they left Mountainview, Meghan decided to walk around looking for employment opportunities. Wolfeboro was one of the wealthiest villages on the lake. They had the highest year round population so Meghan felt confident that somewhere there would be someone who needed some part time help.

As Meghan and Lindy walked down Main Street, both sides of the road were dotted with tourist shops. There were the bakeries, a cookie specialty shop, coffee shops, a donut house, a toy store and a variety of clothing stores that carried everything from infant sizes through adults. You could buy preppy New England styled clothes for yourself, your kids, your grandmother and even your dog. The possibilities seemed endless.

There were stores that rented all kinds of equipment to use on the lake from scuba diving equipment to sailboats. There were stores that rented out bicycles and mopeds by the hour and stores that rented out tour guides by the hour. This town pretty much covered everything. If it needed to be rented, they rented it. If you wanted to buy it, they sold it. Wolfeboro was a happening place.

Meghan smiled when she saw the sign for Mo's Moped Rental. Mo was a big African American man the size of Paul Bunyan. He had a heart the size of Texas and was always helping someone somewhere with something. He was one of the kindest men Meghan knew and lucky for her and Lindy, Mo had taken them under his wing years ago. He watched out for them, sent food their way and always directed any customers seeking a water taxi her way.

As they approached the door of Mo's, Meghan spotted the big man in the driveway giving moped lessons to an elderly lady. "Now listen," Mo said gently, "I want my bike back in one piece and I want you back in one piece. Always wear your helmet," he placed the white helmet on the silver blue head, "and just because the bike will do thirty doesn't mean she has to. She's not begging for more speed. She's a woman advanced in years like you. Treat her like a lady, and she'll keep you happy."

After a few more instructions, the lady was on her way. Mo shook his head as she ran over the curb going out of the driveway. "She's going to kill herself," he muttered. "At eighty years old, she decides she wants to learn to ride a moped. I should have never let her get on the bike."

"She'll have fun," Meghan smiled as she watched the lady zoom down the road.

"Just how long have you been standing there?" Mo threw his big hands on his hips.

Meghan laughed. "We pretty much watched the whole show."

"She's going to hurt herself," Mo shook his head.

"Maybe she's a natural."

Mo frowned at Meghan. "Are we talking about the same lady that just ran over the curb on the way out of my driveway?"

Meghan laughed. "Yeah, we're talking about the same lady. Hey, she didn't fall off the bike." Meg shrugged. "That's a good start."

"I'm not going to stop worrying about granny until she rolls back into my driveway."

"She might surprise you."

"She might come back all bruised up with the bike trashed, too. You know," Mo laughed, "it's harder for me to convince tourists to rent the bike once it's been trashed. It's definitely not good for business."

"They are so fussy," Meghan teased.

"You know it," his loud laugh floated through the air. "So, what brings you two to town today?"

"We just convinced Mountainview to buy ten dozen eggs a week from my chickens!" Lindy stated proudly.

Mo smiled. "Man, you have got yourself some mighty busy chickens. You're quite a little businesswoman, Lindy. I am truly impressed." He reached down and shook her hand.

Lindy beamed. Mo was one of the few men around that took the time to notice Lindy. He was like a father figure to both of them, and his compliments and encouraging words were like medicine to a wounded heart.

"So," Mo grinned at Lindy, "do you think that you might be able to bring me some of your fresh eggs? I love eggs for breakfast."

Lindy frowned. "I can't. I sold all my eggs to Mrs. Matthews at Mountainview."

Mo pretended to be shocked. "That Mrs. Matthews is taking all your eggs?"

Lindy nodded. "It's OK because she's paying for them."

"Well, I hope so." Mo winked at Lindy. "You know, I guess if I'm going to have some of your eggs, I'll just have to trick that Mrs. Matthews. I'll head over there for breakfast and get her to cook them for me. Now that's a good deal."

"Hey, Mo," Meghan as curiously, "you wouldn't know anyone looking for help in town, would you?"

Mo grinned. "Why, I just might. What are you looking to do?"

"Almost anything. I need a job," Meghan shrugged. "With the water taxi customers gone for the season, I need to find something to fill in the gap."

"I think Meghan should get a job doing something with food so that we can work and eat." It was obvious that Lindy was quite pleased with her idea.

Mo's eyes narrowed as he looked at her intensely. "Are you getting enough food to eat?" He had known in the past that there had been plenty of times that they hadn't.

"Yes, we are," Meg reassured him. "We're fine."

Mo frowned. "Now, are you saying you're fine because you really are fine or are you saying that you're fine because you don't want to talk about it anymore."

Meghan had to laugh. Mo knew her too well, and there was no fooling the man. "Ever since I picked up the paper route and Lindy started her eggs route, we've been fine. We actually eat three meals a day."

"Like you should," Mo muttered. "Now, what are you going to do in the off season?"

Meghan was aware that Mo was watching her closely. "That's why I'm here looking for a job. I figured that since Wolfsboro is busy year around, there has to be some place that I can work after school and on weekends." Meghan hesitated. "The only tough thing is, I will have Lindy with me."

"I'm going to work, too!" Lindy added excitedly.

"I'm sure you will," Mo winked at the energetic little girl.

"I'll tell you what," Mo smiled, "I just might be able to help you out. My wife just lost her part timer because she went back to college." Mo paused and he looked at Lindy. " I'm just not sure that you'd like to work at the Chocolate Soldier because you'd have to work around candy all day. You don't like candy, do you?"

"I love candy!" Lindy shouted. "I eat some every day."

Mo laughed loudly. "Well, than, working at the Chocolate Soldier might be good for you." Mo glance at Meg. "I suppose you like working with candy, too?"

"That's sounds like a dream job."

"You can't eat everything, you know."

Meghan laughed. "If I ate everything, I wouldn't fit out the door."

Mo smiled. "I never comment on a woman and her weight. It's never my business and I don't plan on ever making it my business." Mo winked at Meghan. "Why don't we take a walk up the road and talk to my wife?"

As the three of them entered the Chocolate Soldier, the sleigh bells on the door jingled announcing their arrival. The smell of chocolate assaulted the girls' noses and had their mouths instantly watering. Meghan smiled. This place could be heaven to work in or pure torture.

"Her store smells a lot better than mine, don't you think?" Mo grinned at the girls.

"She sells chocolate. Chocolate smells almost better than anything else." Meghan eyed a candy bar near her and shoved her hands in her pockets so she didn't devour it.

"Then this job is for you." Mo nodded.

Mrs. Mo came around the corner at that moment and looked very pleased to see her unexpected visitors. Meghan didn't miss the loving way that Mo and Mrs. Mo smiled at each other. She hoped someday she would have someone to smile at like that.

"Hi, Sugar," Mo looked like a boy in love. "Meghan and Lindy are looking for part-time work. They can work every Saturday and every day after school. Do you think you've got any openings for them?"

Mrs. Mo smiled kindly at the girls. "Well, it looks like you two are my angels. I just lost Carol to college last week, and I've been going crazy trying to do everything. When can you start?"

"Both of us?" Meghan question.

"Yes, I'll hire both of you, Meg. I'll pay you minimum wage to start, and Lindy," Mrs. Mo leaned down toward the girl, "I'll give you three dollars an hour to vacuum and help your sister stock shelves. Does that sound fair?"

"That sounds more than fair," Meghan felt the offer was too generous.

"Meg," Mo leaned down and whispered in her ear, "take the deal. You don't want to hurt Mrs. Mo's feelings."

"I don't want to take advantage of her either."

"Take the deal," he instructed again.

"When do we start?" Meghan looked anxiously at Mrs. Mo.

"How about right now?"

"That sounds good to me." Meghan glanced at Mo and then Mrs. Mo. "Thank you. I appreciate this so much. We won't let you down."

Mrs. Mo put an arm around Meghan's shoulder. "You could never let us down. You're like one of our own. Now come with me girls and I'll show you around."

"Hey, now, don't I get a kiss for bringing you new employees?" Mo grinned at his wife.

Mrs. Mo went over and kissed her husband on the check. "Thank you, dear. Help yourself to a candy bar on the way out."

"Yes, Ma'am," Mo beamed. Meghan loved the way Mo cherished his wife. He made no secret of the fact that he was crazy about her. It was precious to see.

"Just one," she turned around and warned him firmly.

"But I brought you two employees. Don't I get a candy bar for each one?"

Mrs. Mo shook her head. "I have to watch him like a hawk," she said to the girls. "Just look at the size of that man. He'd eat all my inventory in one hour if I let him." Mo made a funny face at the girls, grabbed his candy bar and left.

"Now, I'm going to teach you the chocolate business. First rule," Mrs. Mo laughed, "don't eat all your stock. If you do, you'll go out of business quickly. The rule around here is, you can help yourself to one candy bar after school and two on Saturdays."

For the next few hours, the girls worked with Mrs. Mo. Lindy took her job extremely serious. She became a proud vacuum machine operator. Not a speck of dirt was left on the floor when she was done.

Meghan was shown how to operate the cash register and how to keep the shelves shocked. Mrs. Mo carried a wide assortment of candy. She had dark chocolate, milk chocolate, white chocolate and a wonderful mix of all three. You could buy chocolate in fancy gold foil boxes or you could buy chocolate individually. Meghan quickly figured out that buying the chocolate individually was cheaper. You paid more for the fancy gold foil box. Meghan laughed.

Since she couldn't eat the fancy gold foil box it was of no use to her. Meghan smiled. God had given her a job in chocolate heaven.

At five o'clock sharp, Mr. Mo was waiting for them. "Well, ladies, how did your first day go?"

The girls smiled. "I got to vacuum," Lindy was proud of her work.

"You did a fine job." Mo glanced at Meghan. "How about you? Did you have a good day?"

"I had a great day. I don't think you can have a bad day when you're working around chocolate all day."

"Working for Mrs. Mo does have some great perks."

"She lets us eat chocolate," Lindy smiled.

"She does?" Mo acted surprised.

Lindy nodded. "She gave me a chocolate bar to take home too."

Mo looked at his wife. "Can I have one?"

"You had one," she laughed.

"Yes, but it seems so long ago."

"No," Mrs. Mo laughed at her husband.

"Please." Meghan noticed that Mo could beg better than anyone she knew. He really got dramatic in his pleas.

"Listen," she waved at hand at him, "maybe if you're a really good boy I'll let you have another one."

"I am always a good boy," Mo smiled. "I'm the best. Now come out here and see what I'm about to do."

The three of them followed Mo out to the parking lot. "You drove the Banana here?" Meghan smiled at the bright yellow station wagon that had been tagged as the Banana years ago. Mo kept his baby in great shape and often referred to the car as rolling sunshine.

"I am loaning you this fine piece of machinery," Mo leaned casually on the roof of the yellow car as he spoke. "You are going to need a car to get from Weir's Beach to Wolfsboro."

"We take the boat from Cedar Island to Wolfeboro. It's quicker."

"What are you going to do when it rains or snows?"

Meghan shrugged. "We still take the boat. It's the only transportation we have."

"Well not any more," Mo grinned at her. "I'm loaning you the Banana. You can keep it as long as you need it."

"Mo," Meghan felt at a loss for words, "this is your baby. It's too much."

Mo smiled. "You need a car. I know you'll take care of her." Mo took a step closer to Meghan. "What do you do when the lake freezes over? How do you get into town to buy groceries? And for that matter, how do you get to school or the doctor's?" Mo was frowning now and Meghan knew his frown would deepen once he heard her answer.

"I ride my scooter or I get a ride with Daniel Hatch."

Mo sighed. "Stupid boy," he mumbled. "We both know that's no longer an option for you. Take the car."

"I feel like it's too much."

"Now listen here, Meghan Kane, I have given this a lot of thought. Even before you came to town today, I was planning on loaning you the Banana. I don't like to watch you and Lindy doubling up on your scooter. When you fly by my shop at forty miles an hour, I have a cardiac arrest."

"The scooter only does thirty," Meghan grinned.

"Don't sass me, girl," Mo waved a finger at her. "You know well enough what I mean."

"We wear helmets."

"That's going to do you a whole lot of good when you wipe out on the snow and ice this winter. Please," he urged as he put the keys in Meghan's hand, "take the Banana. She'll be good to you, and you'll get safely where you need to go."

Meghan looked over at Mrs. Mo. "Are you sure?"

Mrs. Mo smiled gently. "He's been talking about it for a long time. We both worry about you girls. This will give us one less thing to worry about."

Meghan's eyes teared up, and she went over and gave Mr. and Mrs. Mo a big hug. Their caring and generosity touched her deeply. God had provided people along the way to watch out for her and Lindy, and no one did more than the Mo's. They continually overwhelmed her with love. She often felt like they were her guardian angels. "I'll take care of her," Meghan whispered.

"You'd better," Mo teased. "I realize that it's kind of late to ask you this, but do you have your driver's license?"

Meghan took the license out of her wallet and handed it to Mo. He studied it carefully. "Are you sure this picture is you? I don't think it looks a thing like you." He howled with laughter as Meg smacked him in the arm.

"Don't speed," he warned as he handed her license back to her.

"I won't."

"Don't pick up any hitchhikers."

"I wouldn't think of it," Meghan answered dramatically.

Mo shot her a hard look. "Good. Now, you need to drive slow when we're having weather."

Meghan laughed. "Mo, we're always having weather."

He narrowed his eyes at her. "There you go, sassing me again. What I meant was, you need to drive slow when we're having bad weather. Even a wet road can shoot you into the lake."

"I'll remember that," Meghan grinned. Driver's Ed. with Mo was too funny.

Lindy laughed and Mo looked at her. "Do you have something to add to this conversation?"

Lindy smiled. "Meghan has never driven before except to get her license."

Mo's mouth dropped open. "Say it isn't so!"

Meghan laughed. "Do you want the keys back?"

Mo paused and let a low whistle fill her ears. "No," he grabbed her hand, "but you and I are going for some driving lessons right now. Get behind the wheel."

"What do you know about driving?" Mo asked as he slid into the passenger seat beside her.

Meghan laughed. "Let's see. Never speed, never pick up hitchhikers and watch out for bad weather because it can shoot you into the lake."

His eyes narrowed as he recognized the same speech he had just given her. "That isn't funny."

"I've never really driven before."

"That isn't funny, either," he whispered more to himself than to her.

"Oh, there's a few other things that I know." Meghan put her hand on the horn and blasted it. "That's the horn, and that's the radio." She pointed to the old radio. Mrs. Mo and Lindy laughed, but Mr. Mo just stared at her. He looked like he was trying hard not to laugh. "What more does a teenager need to know?"

"Give me those keys," Mo laughed. "I think I just changed my mind."

Meghan laughed. "I passed the written part of my driver's test with a ninety five and the road part with a ninety-four."

"What did you get wrong?"

Meghan sighed. "Can you believe that they actually expect you to stop at all the stop signs and slow down for all the pedestrians? I think it's ridiculous myself. The pedestrians should learn to run a little bit faster when they see a car coming. Honestly, it's so unfair to the drivers. All they have you doing is stopping and slowing down. How am I ever supposed to get anywhere if I have to stop and slow down all the time?"

"Get out of my car," Mo grumbled.

"I thought it was my car?" Meghan laughed.

"Not anymore."

"I'm a good driver," Meghan protested.

"Here's the thing," Mo grinned. "In order to be a good driver you need to drive."

"That's why I need the Banana."

"I'm going to teach you to drive right now, but first you're going to be in the passenger seat."

"I've mastered the passenger seat. I've been doing it for sixteen years."

"Don't sass me Meghan. Move over and let the master show you how it's done." Mo spent the next two hours giving Meghan a crash course on driving. They drove the back roads, the highway and even practiced parallel parking.

"Well, I think you're ready." Mo smiled at Meghan. "Be good to my baby."

"I will. I promise."

Mo leaned over and hugged Meghan. "We love you girls like our own. Anytime you need anything you'd better not hesitate to ask."

Meghan tried to fight back her tears. "Thank you Mo. Lindy and I love you and Mrs. Mo too."

As Meghan and Lindy drove the Banana towards Weir's Beach, she thanked the Lord for Mo and his wife. They had looked out for her and Lindy since her mother had left them. They were always there for them and they were the ones that Meg turned to in times of trouble without feeling embarrassed or ashamed.

If they spotted the need before Meghan did, they would take care of the need quietly before she had to ask. They were special and she loved them like parents. Once again, God had proven himself to be unbelievably good to her and Lindy. He amazed her at how He took care of her and brought special people like the Mo's into her life. He truly was the father to the fatherless.

Twenty-One

*S*omehow Meghan wasn't surprised to see Daniel Hatch at the Wharf at Weir's Beach. She parked the Banana and sat and stared at Daniel for a full minute. As if he knew he was being spied on, he slowly turned around and searched the area behind him. Once he spotted Meghan, they stared at each other for a moment.

Meghan felt assaulted by a rush of emotional memories every time she saw Daniel. She wasn't sure when the roller coaster ride that she was on was going to end. She knew in her heart that Daniel was on the same ride. They had known each other too long and too well not to be seriously affected by the break up.

"Are we going to sit here all day?" Lindy complained. " I want to get home and tell dad about the Banana."

Meghan got out of the car and made sure the Banana was locked up for the night. As she slowly, almost regretfully made her way to the docks, she couldn't help but watch Daniel working with his father. It was as if someone had rewound her life for a minute to a happier, more pleasant time.

Daniel was helping his father ready the mail boat for tomorrow's route. All the evening preparations that they did, like sorting the mail and stocking up on the snack bar items helped them to keep the Sally G. on schedule.

"I'm going to marry him someday," Lindy whispered in a dreamy voice.

"You can have him," Meghan couldn't hide the anger in her voice.

"You don't like Daniel anymore?"

Meghan sighed loudly. "Not like I used to."

"Hey," Daniel greeted them as he hopped down from the Sally G. onto the dock. "How's it going?"

Meghan bit back her temper. What right did he have to ask her anything? The man had crushed her heart to bits and it irritated her to no end that he often acted like nothing happened between them. Meghan leveled him with a hard look. "It's going just fine."

Before their conversation had much of a chance to begin or end, Sheriff Stewart came walking toward them. "Meghan, I want you to know that I made sure that your mom made it out of town last week. It seems she's been living in New York City."

Meghan glanced at Daniel's face long enough for her to notice his shocked expression. Mr. Hatch had heard the Sheriff, and he immediately jumped down from the mail boat onto the docks. "Meghan," Mr. Hatch stated in alarm, "you're mother came back?"

Meghan slowly nodded. "Last week." She glanced at Lindy who was playing on the other end of the dock and prayed that the little girl wouldn't hear any part of the conversation.

"Your mother came back, and you never bothered to tell me?" Daniel's voice was rising quickly.

"I dealt with it," Meg answered firmly.

"Didn't you think that I would want to know?" Daniel looked both hurt and angry at the same time.

"I didn't think it was any of your business."

Mr. Hatch stepped between them. "What did she want, Meg?"

"I'm not really sure," Meghan shrugged, "but my guess would be money. The only time she ever came back was when she was looking for money."

"It's a good thing that I was on the docks that morning," Jimmy looked at Meghan protectively, "her mom was getting ready to hit her right before I stepped in."

"Is that true?" Daniel demanded angrily.

"Nothing happened," Meg tried to dismiss the incident calmly. She found that the longer she and Daniel were separated, the quicker her blood boiled when she was around him.

"Something could have happened," he took a step closer to her.

"Yeah, well, it didn't." Meghan's voice warned Daniel to trend carefully. "Let it go, Daniel. It's not your concern anymore."

"Is it Reid's concern?" His accusing tone of voice really ticked her off.

"That is none of your business."

"I'll take that as a yes," he stated with annoying calmness in his voice. "So, you'll share your life with the Perfect Prince, but not with a lifelong friend like me."

"Reid is not the Perfect Prince anymore. He's changed."

Daniel smiled smugly. "I find it very interesting that you're defending him." Daniel stared at her a minute. "You've fallen for him, haven't you?"

He had pushed her too far, and the steam blowing out of her ears should have warned him of that fact. "Yes, Daniel, I like Reid Kensington very much. In fact," she stepped right up to him so she was almost in his face, "I think that I may even love him. He's sincere, honest, compassionate and doesn't play games with me like you did."

As Meghan went to push past Daniel to get to her boat, he grabbed her arm to stop her. "I loved you," he said strongly.

Meghan glared at him. He was still playing games, and she wasn't going to be a part of it. "That's right, Daniel," Meghan said between clenched teeth, "you loved me. That's past tense just like our relationship."

"We can still have a future," he begged.

"Just then a shrill voice cut through the air. "Daniel, oh Daniel, I'm so glad that you're still here." Brittany came bouncing across the boardwalk and down to the docks. She was wearing a tight pink halter top and a short white mini skirt."

"Oh," she slithered between Meghan and Daniel much like a snake would have, "I was hoping that we were still on for tonight. I think this is going to be the best party yet." Brittany turned and looked Meghan in the eye. "Everyone that is anyone is going to be there." She cast a disgusted look at Lindy like she was road kill. "No loser allowed—even little kid losers."

Something in Meghan snapped. "You're going to have to get changed before your party." Her voice addressed Brittany with all the softness of a bulldozer.

"Oh, what do you know?" She took a bold step closer to Meghan. "This is the latest fashion of the season. Do you honestly think that I'm going to take fashion tips from someone who considers Chap Stick a major makeup accessory product?"

"Maybe you should take a tip from someone who doesn't let anyone push her or her sister around."

"Oh, and what tip could you give me, thrift shop girl?"

"That going to a party wet is not cool." Meghan gently pushed Brittany backwards and watched as she teetered for a moment on her white Go-Go boots. An expression of panic covered the Malibu Barbie's face before she fell backward into the lake.

When Brittany's blonde head surfaced, she immediately began to whine about the unfairness of the situation. "I warned you before never to pick on my sister or me. I said if you ever did that you'd be sorry. Are you sorry, Brit?"

"I can't believe you did that," Daniel's mouth had dropped open in shock.

"Someone should have dumped her in the lake a long time ago."

"That's true," Daniel whispered quietly, "I just didn't think you'd be the one to do it."

"You're right. I shouldn't have been the one to do it. You should have. You should have defended our lifelong friendship. You didn't defend Lindy and me at the beach party, and you didn't defend us now."

"I'm sorry. I really do care."

"You care about yourself."

"I'm not perfect."

Meghan snorted. "No kidding."

"If you want to talk about your mother, call me."

Meghan's face scrunched up in disbelief. "You have got to be kidding. Why would I ever call you?"

"I'm here for you, Meg."

"You haven't been here for me for a long time Daniel. If I want to talk about my mother I'll call my real friends like Reid, Simon, Natasha and Web."

"Don't shut me out."

"Daniel, you shut yourself out."

"Let me back in," he begged. "I'll do anything."

"Daniel, the fact that you're still dating Brittany tells me where you're at. I will never open my heart up to you again." With that said, Meghan pushed past Daniel, called out to Lindy and they both got in their boat and left. She wondered just how long it would take for Daniel to really understand. He had let her go and he would never get her back again.

Twenty-Two

As Meghan drove Lindy and Web in the Banana towards Wolfeboro, she watched Web curiously out of the corner of her eye. "What are you doing?"

"Nothing," Web replied too quickly to make a convincing case.

"It looks to me like Webster's trying to hide." Lindy had leaned forward in the back seat so she could get a good view of him.

"Web..." Meghan drew the single word out, "what is up with you?"

"Nothing." He tried once again to sound convincing but unfortunately for him, Meghan could see right through it.

Meghan's eyes narrowed. "You're embarrassed to be seen in the Banana."

"No, I'm not." The fact that he scrunched down further in the seat as they passed a group of teens did nothing to help his case.

"Yes you are." Meghan was torn between irritation and laughter. He looked so ridiculous. "If you sink any lower in the seat, you'll be sitting on the floor."

Webster sighed loudly. "Listen, I'm going through a very insecure time in my teenage life. I'm overly self-conscious and overly concerned with what others think. My hormones are raging out of control." Web glanced at Meghan hesitantly. "I think I may even be starting to like Natasha."

Meghan laughed. "Web, you have liked Natasha since the beginning of last summer."

"That may be true but I am only now willing to admit that fact. I believe I was living in denial."

Meghan laughed again. "We'll get back to Natasha in a minute. First, let's finish the conversation about my car."

"Everybody knows that Banana all over the lake. No one else has a yellow car that's so bright it actually glows in the dark."

"It's a nice cheery car." Meghan beeped the horn and waved at some friends.

"Don't do that!" Web pleaded.

Meghan glanced at him. "You know, you're pathetic when you beg. It isn't becoming to you at all." Meghan beeped the horn again and waved at Miss Brinkle, the town librarian.

"Please don't do that."

"Do what?" Meghan acted obvious.

"Meghan Kane," Web growled out, "you know exactly what I'm talking about."

"The horn?" Meghan grinned as she tooted it again.

"Yes, the horn!" Webster sounded completely exasperated as he tried to sink lower in his seat. "I am trying hard not to draw attention to myself."

"I noticed." Meghan cast a quick glance at Web, "You know, if I had known that you were going to sit on the floor, I would have let Lindy sit up front."

"Knock it off."

"I really wish you would, Web. I'm sorry that you don't like my car."

"That's not entirely true."

"What part?"

"I like your car; I'd just like it better if it wasn't painted screaming yellow."

"I'm not changing the color."

"I know. I know. I'm trying to adjust."

Meghan looked at Web, and then smiled as she beeped and waved at Natasha coming out of the grocery store. "Have you no sympathy at all?"

"No. None at all." Meghan and Lindy howled.

"That was Natasha!" Web's voice bordered on sheer panic.

"That's right!" Meghan patted Web on the leg. "We were going to talk about her next, but we might want to wait."

"Why?" Web had sunk below the dashboard.

"She's coming over to say hi."

"No!" Meghan took pity on the fear that she saw in Web's eyes.

"Get a grip. Come on," she patted on the seat. "You're going to want to get up here before she comes over."

Web groaned and climbed back up into the seat. He tried to appear casual as Natasha approached the car, but Meg could tell that he was on the verge of a nervous breakdown.

"Hey, Meghan," Natasha greeted warmly, "how's it going?"

"Great, and you?"

"Pretty good. Oh, hi, Lindy. How are you doing?"

"Web's acting weird."

Nat glanced at him. "Is he really?"

"Yes." The little girl did not understand what Web was going through.

When Natasha turned her brown eyes on Webster, he broke out into a sweat. "Webster, are you OK? You don't look so good."

"I told you, he's acting weird." Lindy repeated her earlier diagnosis.

"I think he's got a bug," Meghan added sympathetically. She didn't bother to mention she thought he had been bitten by the love bug. Somehow she knew that Nat knew that.

"Maybe you need some fresh air." Natasha looked closely at Web. "Do you want to walk for a bit?"

Web's face paled, and he looked at Meghan with terror in his eyes. "He's going to help Mo this morning." Meg tried to help her friend out.

"We can walk from here to there." Nat wasn't about to give up. "It's only a couple of blocks. The walk would do you good."

When Web didn't respond, Natasha went around to the passenger door and yanked it open. "Webster T. Long," she commanded, "get out of the car."

Web shook his head no. He couldn't even look at her.

"Webster, in case no one's told you, I don't bite. Now, get out of the car."

"I'm staying," Web whimpered.

"Oh, no, you're not," Natasha had more fight in her than Web had in him. "All summer long you have gone out of your way to avoid me. I want to be your friend Webster, not date you. You don't need to worry, because I can't go out on a date until I'm out of high school." Natasha looked at Meghan and shrugged her shoulders. "My parent's rules…." She turned back to Web. "I've made up my mind that we're going to be friends. Now out." She waved her hand and Web followed it with his big fearful eyes.

Web looked at Meghan as if he were having a heart attack. "You'd better just go." Meg whispered. "She's not going to take no for an answer." Meghan gave Web a little push, and he practically fell out of the open door. Meg knew this situation was doing little to help Web's sensitive male ego.

"Make sure he gets to Mo's," Meghan instructed Natasha. "Mo's expecting him in half an hour."

"No problem," Nat winked at her friend. "Maybe by that time I'll even get Mr. Long here to talk to me."

As Meghan drove off, she smiled at the scene in her rearview mirror. Natasha and Web were slowly making their way down the sidewalk toward town. Web was walking so stiffly that he looked like a mannequin. Meghan shook her head.

"What's wrong with Webster?" Lindy had turned around and stared at the couple on the sidewalk.

"Love makes people do funny things."

Lindy's face crunched up. "Then I don't think I ever want to be in love."

"I thought you loved Daniel?" Meghan teased.

"Oh, yeah, Daniel. I'll be in love with Daniel, but no one else."

"Why's that?" Meghan asked curiously.

"Because I'm going to marry Daniel. I guess if love makes me funny around him that's OK."

At the traffic light at Main Street and Lake Shore Drive, Meghan took the opportunity to turn in her seat and talk to Lindy. "So, you'll be staying with Mrs. Mo until I get back. OK?"

Lindy nodded. "Mrs. Mo says I'm the best vacuum person that she's ever hired."

"Yes, you are," Meghan smiled. "So you be extra good for her. I'll be back after I talk to a lady."

"'Bout what?" Lindy asked curiously.

"Lots of stuff, Lindy. You don't need to worry about it. I'll be back for you in a hour."

After Meghan dropped Lindy off at the Chocolate Soldier, she turned left onto South Shore Drive and reluctantly headed for her appointment. At that moment, she was so close to hating Reid Kensington. Why in the world had she agreed to go for counseling anyways? Reid was paying for it but she felt like she was paying a much higher price. Having to open her heart up to a perfect stranger about her private life seemed too much to ask.

As she stared at the little white cottage right on the water, she seriously considered not going in. If she was going to bale, now was the time and she would have to act quickly.

She continued staring at the office, knowing just inside the cottage door was Child Psychologist Dr. Mary Martin. Meghan shook her head. What had she gotten herself into? She was no good at talking to people. How was this ever going to work?

She closed her eyes and sighed loudly. She could just picture Dr. Mary Martin in her mind. She was probably one hundred years old, wore her gray hair in a tight bun at the back of her head, and squinted at her patients through oversized gray granny glasses that she rested on the tip of her long, pointed nose.

A head popped out of the front door, and a young woman waved Meghan in. She cringed. Now that she had been spotted, she would have to make an appearance. As she slowly trudged toward the white cottage, she could hear the sound of water gently lapping against the land. She stopped and stared out at the lake for a minute. In her mind, she was already planning the great escape. She needed to come up with a prime excuse as to why she could not stay, and she needed to come up with it quickly.

As she walked through the front door, a voice called to her. "Come back on the porch."

Meghan walked through the small house to where the young woman was standing. She looked around. The good thing about being on the porch was that it was outside and outside would make it easier to escape.

"Have a seat," the woman offered casually.

Meghan dropped down into a brown rocking chair. "Am I early?"

The young woman smiled. "If you're Meghan Kane, then you're right on time."

Meg glanced nervously around looking for an old lady to come hobbling through the door. "What are you looking for?" the woman asked her curiously.

"Where's Dr. Martin?"

The woman smiled again. "I am Dr. Mary Martin."

Meghan's face registered so much shock that Dr. Martin laughed quietly. "Am I different than you expected?" All Meghan could do was nod. "You probably thought I was going to be some old lady, right?"

"Kind of," Meg mumbled

"Everybody does," Dr. Martin laughed again. "I'm only thirty-two. I'm not exactly old enough to get my sunshine card yet."

Meghan smiled. Despite her previous plans to escape, she knew she was going to stay. Dr. Mary Martin was someone that she hadn't expected. She was beautiful, athletic looking and Meg could already sense that she was funny. She found herself wanting to stay, if for no other reason than to see what this dark-haired beauty was going to do next.

She didn't have to wait long. Dr. Martin went into the kitchen and grabbed something from the frig. When she came back, she set two fruit drinks, a plate of sandwiches, and a plate of chocolate cookies on a small table between them.

Meghan eyed the food eagerly. She had skipped breakfast, and her stomach was reminding her of it. "What's this?" Meg pointed to the food. "Is this your idea of a bribe?"

Dr. Martin laughed. "I have a strict policy not to bribe my patients. I won't make you talk about anything that you don't want to talk about."

"OK," Meghan eyed her closely, "so what's with the food?" She tried not to stare at the plate of chocolate cookies in front of her.

"This," Dr. Martin waved a hand at the food, "is my lunch. My schedule is booked solid today, and if I don't have lunch with you, I'm not going to be able to have it. Do you mind?"

Meghan laughed. "You put chocolate cookies in front of me and asked me if I mind? Are you kidding?"

"So, you're a chocolate fan?"

"Big time!" Meghan grinned. "I'd eat anything that's chocolate. I even work at the Chocolate Soldier."

Dr. Martin grinned. "I think I'm jealous."

As they began to eat their sandwiches, Meghan relaxed enough to check out her surroundings. There was a huge Red Sox banner hanging off the porch. Meghan laughed and shook her head at it.

"Are you a baseball fan?"

"Yes," Meg nodded and smiled.

"Do you like the Red Sox?"

"They're OK from a distance. Being a Red Sox fan is too much of a roller coaster ride for me. Every year is the year that they're going to win the World Series. Every year is the year that they're going to go all the way."

Dr. Martin laughed. "I hear you but I still root for them. I can't help it." She paused and took a sip from her pink fruit drink. "Just don't tell me that you like the New York Yankees. I can deal with anything but Yankee fans."

Meghan laughed. "Well, maybe I should leave before things get ugly."

Dr. Martin sat upright in her chair. "You like the Yankees?"

"I love them!" Meghan practically shouted. "I started watching baseball with my dad when I was five. It was one of the few subjects that we connected on. When we couldn't talk about life's problems and the things that were bothering us, we could always talk about baseball. Somehow it seemed to be a common ground for us."

"That's good," Dr. Martin nodded thoughtfully. "Who's your favorite player?"

"Don Mattingly, first base champion and grand slam slugger."

"He's a great player." Dr. Martin paused. "I can see that we're going to have to agree to disagree here."

"No problem," Meghan grinned.

"I'd just like to say that Boston has a lot of great players."

"That's true," Meghan grabbed a cookie off the plate, "it must be really hard for them being on a losing team all the time. Always getting close to the World Series but never walking away with the ring."

"OK," Dr. Martin narrowed her eyes at Meg, "we are definitely going to have to agree to disagree before this conversation becomes immature and insulting."

Meghan laughed and shook her head. "So what do you want to talk about now?"

Dr. Martin smiled. "I was thinking that I should tell you a little about myself." Meghan nodded. "First of all, even though the name on the door says Dr. Martin, I prefer that you call me Mary. I'm more comfortable with it."

Meghan nodded. "OK."

"What do you want to be called?"

"Everyone calls me Meghan or Meg."

"Do you like being called that?"

"Yeah," Meg smiled, "if you called me something else, I probably wouldn't respond. I'd think you were talking to someone else."

"OK," Mary nodded thoughtfully. "I'm glad that Reid sent you my way. We have more things in common than you think."

"Not baseball," Meghan smiled.

"No, not baseball, but there are other things in life than baseball."

Meg laughed. "That's true. So, what else do we have in common?"

"Well, for starters, my mother left my dad, my little brother and me when I was young. When my parents got a divorce, she made no secret of the fact that she didn't want us."

"Really?" Meghan was on the edge of her chair. This story was sounding too familiar.

"Yeah," Mary continued, "she didn't even fight for custody of my bother or me because she didn't want us. You know, even now, after all these years it still hurts to talk about it."

"I'm sorry," Meg said sincerely. She felt like she needed to change the subject, because she could relate to Mary's situation better than she wanted to. "Where are you from?"

Mary smiled at the sudden change of subject. "I'm a Jersey girl she said easily.

"You're from New Jersey?"

"Yeah," Mary replied in a reminiscing voice, "I grew up on the shore."

Meghan laughed. "How did you ever get to be a Red Sox fan living next door to New York?"

Mary grinned. "How did you ever get to be a Yankees fan living next door to Boston?"

Meghan laughed again. Mary was nothing that she had ever expected. She wasn't stiff or overly seriously. She was fun and spunky and knew how to throw the lines right back at her. "I deserved that."

"Yes you did!" Mary laughed. "I guess I was a bit of a rebel. All my friends were crazy about the New York Yankees. I really became a die-hard Red Sox fan when I saw Yaz play. Have you ever heard of him?"

"I've heard of him. He's a legend in baseball. Didn't he used to play first base for the Sox?"

Mary nodded. "He had a killer swing and a killer smile. It was love at first sight for me." She looked at Meghan and laughed. "He was really something to watch."

Meghan laughed. "I guess I'll have to take your word on that. He played before my time."

"Are you saying that I'm old?" Mary laughed.

"Not as old as I thought you'd be. You're OK."

Mary shook her head. "Well, I'm glad you think so."

As they continued to eat their lunch, Meghan grabbed a chocolate cookie off the plate. "These are great!"

"Thanks but I can't take credit for them. I picked them up at the Gingerbread House."

"That's my favorite bakery."

"Mine, too. Man, their stuff is way too good. I can't seem to go into town without stopping at the Gingerbread House and the Chocolate Soldier. I'm going to gain a hundred pounds by Christmas if I'm not careful."

"I know the feeling."

A serious expression covered Mary's face, and Meghan waited for the speech that she knew she was about to hear. "Meg, I'm going to share with you something and I'd appreciate it if you kept it between us. Well," Mary paused, "Reid knows too. You can tell him whatever you choose to from our sessions."

"OK," Meghan leaned forward anxiously.

"Meg, the reason that my dad divorced my mom was because he caught my mom abusing me."

"No," the simple word came out in a soft, unbelieving whisper.

Mary nodded her head. "She had been abusing me for a long time and I was too embarrassed and too ashamed to say anything."

"I'm so sorry." Meghan bit her lip to keep from crying.

"My father made a deal with my mother," Mary went on in a quiet voice, "that if she agreed to give him full custody, he wouldn't press charges." Mary sighed. "You know, after all these years it still hurts to talk about it. I suspect it always will."

"Have you seen your mother since?"

Mary shook her head. "No, and to be honest with you, I don't want to see her. We never had those warm, fuzzy memories that many children share with their mothers. She was an alcoholic, and the alcohol consumed her. Whenever I was with her, from my earliest memory, I was always on the abusing end. There were no good times or any memory lanes that I want to reminisce about. I think I tried so hard to forget about it. Remembering is the last thing I wanted to do, seeing her would be the next."

"I had no idea."

A faint smiled covered Mary's face. "I told you we had a lot in common."

"I'm sorry that we do," Meghan tone was filled with turbulent emotions.

"So am I, Meg," Mary said gently. "The reason that I'm sharing this with you is that I want you to know that I've been there. I understand the pain, the guilt and the hurt. I've lived through the nightmares for years; and to be honest with you, every once in a while one comes back and blindsides me." Mary paused and took a slow sip of her fruit drink.

"Meg, I want you to know that I'm a survivor; and more importantly, you can be too." She exhaled loudly. "You can't survive something like this on your own. A friend basically forced me to go see a Christian counselor. I learned to deal with my past, and I also became a Christian in the process."

"Meg," Mary reached out and touched her hand, "this is something that you can survive. I have, and with God's help, I can help you. Please," she urged, "let me help you. I have been there and I will take you out of this nightmare."

Meghan studied Mary for a minute. She suddenly realized that Mary was an answer to her prayers that she hadn't even prayed yet. God knew that she needed someone like Mary to help her, and he used Reid to arrange the meeting. Meghan slowly nodded her head. "Thank you," her voice was quieter than a whisper, "I know that I need help."

Mary looked directly into Meghan's eyes. "I won't let you down."

Even though Meghan had only known Mary for less than an hour, she knew that she could trust her. "I know you'll do your best."

"It's not going to be easy. It's actually going to be a long and painful journey."

Meghan sighed. "I know."

"You won't be walking it alone, Meg. You'll have God, Reid and me. I'd say that's a pretty terrific team."

Meghan smiled. "I'd have to agree." The smiled disappeared and was replaced by a look of sheer determination. "I want this to end. I want all of it to end. The nightmares are awful…"

"It will end," Mary reassured her. "You've got to remember that it will take tim, and once in a while those nightmares may come back. In time, you will have less and less of them. God is going to help you, Meghan. He brought you to me on purpose."

"I hope so," Meghan sounded far from convinced.

"Hey," Mary covered Meghan's hand and squeezed it reassuringly. "I know so. You're going to be all right."

As Mary closed the session in prayer, for the first time in years Meghan actually believed what Mary had just said. She somehow felt that God was going to heal her from her past and that she was indeed going to be all right.

Twenty-Three

$\mathcal{R}$eid was waiting for Meghan when she came out of Dr. Mary Martin's office. "How did it go?" He wasted no time with the small talk.

Meghan slowly smiled. "When I walked in there, I was thinking of a hundred different ways that I could ditch the appointment and torture you."

Reid grinned. "I'm not surprised."

"I wasn't crazy at all about spilling my guts to a total stranger."

"I understand." Reid watched her as he rocked back and forth on his heels.

Meghan exhaled loudly. "Well, as we got talking, I quickly realized that we have a lot on common. We have a lot more in common than I'd like. No one likes to have abuse as a common factor."

Reid put an arm around Meg's shoulders. "I understand what you're saying; but on the flip side of things, because she has been down that road, she can help you through it like no one else can."

"That's true."

"So, my idea to see Mary was a good thing?" Reid wanted to make sure that Meghan wasn't still mad at him.

She smiled at him. "Reid, this is one of the best ideas that you've had. If you hadn't pushed me, I guarantee that I wouldn't have come on my own."

"I want to support you, Meghan, in whatever way I can. I want to encourage you, and I want you to lean on me. I want to be the shoulder that you can cry on."

Meghan smiled. "I've already done that. You're a good friend, Reid."

Reid's face became stern. "You must know by know that I don't just want to be friends with you."

Meg stared at the handsome young man for a second. "What is it that you want, Reid?"

Reid took Meghan's hands and wrapped them in his own. "I want you, Meg. I want to be with you for the rest of my life." Reid smiled tenderly at Meghan's shocked expression. "I know that we've only been close for a few months, but I'm a man who knows what he wants." He squeezed her hands lovingly. "What I want is you."

Meghan turned away from his loving eyes. "I'm not ready for that kind of relationship, Reid. Daniel really messed up my heart." She turned and looked at him directly. "I'm not ready for what you're ready for."

Reid smiled tenderly. "I know. I'm willing to wait until the day that you are ready. We will take the slow road, Meg. We can be friends for the next four years if you want. I just needed you to understand where I was coming from."

"I understand," Meg answered quietly, "but I need for us to stay good friends for now."

"For now," he leaned down and kissed her on the cheek as he laced his hands through hers, "but not forever."

"Let's take one step at a time." Meghan tugged Reid's hand toward the sandy beach, and they quietly walked along it, each immersed in their own thoughts.

"One step at a time is fine," Reid agreed, "as long as those steps lead us in the direction of forever. That's where I want to go with you, Meghan. I have never felt this way about any girl before."

"What way is that?"

"That I love you."

Meghan stopped walking and stared at Reid. She was not ready to hear this. "There are as many forms of love out there as there are grains of sand on the beach."

Reid took both her hands in his. "I want you to understand the way that I love you." He paused and looked at her with so much love flowing from his eyes that she felt so cherished and treasured. It was a wonderful feeling. "I love you the way a man loves a woman. I love you in the way that I want to spend the rest of my life with you. I love you like I've never loved another person in my entire life. I want to spend the rest of my life with you and raise a bunch of kids together. I want to wake up each morning at your side and feel the warmth of your body next to me at night. I want to grow old with you and then help raise our grandkids together." Reid leaned down and kissed Meghan on top of her brown hair. "I love you with all of my heart. Now do you understand the kind of love that I'm talking about?"

"Yes," Meghan answered weakly.

Reid smiled at her. "I want to put you before myself, and that's not something that's easy for a Kensington to do. We're kind of a self-absorbed bunch, but I keep thinking of you all day long and find myself looking for opportunities to brighten your today."

Reid put an arm around Meghan's shoulders and guided her down the soft sandy beach. "Meg, I will wait for you from now until the end of time if that's what it takes. You're the first thought I have in the morning, and at night you fill my mind with wonderful dreams. I love you, and I know that I will love you forever."

Meghan smiled at him through tearful eyes. "You won't have to wait that long."

As Reid embraced her in a tender hug, neither one of them noticed Daniel Hatch sitting on the side dock. He had heard every word of Reid's loving declaration, and all he could do was shake his head in disbelief. He had come into Wolfeboro that day to see Meghan. He wanted to share his good news with her. After months of drifting, he had finally broken it off with Brittany Bentley. As he continued to watch Reid and Meghan in a loving hug, it suddenly struck him that Meghan wouldn't be interested in his news.

He quietly slipped off the docks unnoticed and disappeared behind a row of stores. He had asked God for forgiveness, but he knew he still needed to talk to Meghan. He had been such a fool. What they had together was so special. It was the type of love that comes around once in a lifetime. He silently begged God to let him win Meghan back. He loved her, and he needed her. He knew that for sure now, but what he didn't know for sure was that if he would be able to convince Meghan of it.

She was the only girl for him. A troubled sigh escaped him. What if she never came back to him? What if they were truly meant for each other but they never got together again because of foolish choices he had made when he was only sixteen? What if she married the charming, wealthy, handsome Reid Kensington?

Daniel forced all the negative thoughts from his mind. The only thing that he could let his heart focus on was getting Meghan back. He had to win her back. They were meant for each other, and he prayed that God would help Meghan see that. It would be an awful thing for two people that were clearly meant for each other to never get together. Daniel didn't want Meghan to marry the wrong guy. He was the right one for her, and somehow he had to make sure she knew that.

Titles in the New England Novel series
by
Sharon Snow Sirois

Cedar Island

Cedar Island is sheltered in Penny's Cove on beautiful Lake Winnipesaukee. New England's largest lake is nestled into the foothills of the White Mountains of New Hampshire.

Cedar Island follows the story as the people from Penny's Cove grow up and begin their adult lives. Daniel Hatch as taken over his father's position aboard the Sally G. and is now the new U. S. Mail Boat captain on the lake. As he travels to the islands, delivering the mail, his new assistant, Lindy Kane, keeps things lively.

While Lindy is meeting all the island folks and watching Daniel and Reid fight over Meghan, her mind is busy with prenuptial plans.

A secret wedding takes place in the small country chapel on Bethlehem Island. The newlywed couple travels from New Hampshire to Martha's Vineyard, an island off the Massachusetts Cape Cod shoreline. They enjoy visiting the picturesque island; its quaint historical villages, and dining at charming waterfront restaurants. Their days are filled with long romantic walks along Martha's Vineyard's rocky beaches, leisurely picnics and exploring the five lighthouses that surround the island, from Edgartown to West Chop.

When tragedy unexpectedly strikes, the people from Lake Winnipesaukee pray that God will return peace and stability to their small community once again.

Cedar Island will be available at your local bookstore in the fall of 2003.

Sawyer's Crossing

$\mathcal{K}$elly Douglas returns to her hometown to fulfill a lifelong dream of becoming a police officer. Sawyer's Crossing is a small, picturesque Vermont town known for its many covered bridges and quaint New England styled shops.

It is in this close-knit community that Kelly quietly begins to conduct her own investigation into the unsolved murders of her parents. As the shocking truth of the investigation unfolds, Kelly finds herself not only the target of the man she's hunting, but the bait for him as well!

Mark Mitchell, the new police chief of Sawyer's Crossing, is a man that Kelly both admires and fears. He is a determined, dedicated, attractive young man, intent on not only capturing the murderer, but capturing Kelly's heart forever.

As Kelly and Mark unite to solve this crime, painful scars from the past threaten their investigation and their promising future together. Will they allow God to heal the past and replace their pain and fear with His perfect peace and love?

This heart-warming story, with its cast of charming characters, will have you laughing one minute and crying the next. As hope and heartache meet, ordinary people rely on God to solve extraordinary problems. Sawyer's Crossing is a modern-day fairy tale with a happily ever after ending.

Sugar Creek Inn

Sugar Creek is a quiet New England town located on Eagle Lake in Maine. It is a beautiful, relaxing area that is frequented by tourists who enjoy a variety of outdoor activities, such as sailing, swimming, and skiing.

It is here on Eagle Lake that the Miller family runs The Sugar Creek Inn. There is never a dull moment between the four spirited sisters, the two elderly brothers who are permanent house guests, the boyfriend whom everyone loves, the boyfriend whom nobody likes, the regular house guests, and the Miller's two rowdy dogs.

When Matthew Bishop comes to Sugar Creek as the new pastor, things get very complicated for the youngest Miller daughter. Jacilyn Miller is engaged to marry her childhood friend, Bradley Clarke. The wedding plans have been made, invitations ordered, and gowns picked out. Yet Jack's well-ordered world turns upside down as she finds herself attracted to the pastor who's supposed to marry her. The chemistry between Matthew and Jack is so strong it's electrifying. The more Jack tries to stay away from the young pastor, the more they get thrown together.

Jack Miller struggles with her feelings and tries hard to rein in her spinning emotions. As she tries to honor promises made in the past, Matthew challenges her to honor God and His ways above anything else.

Stony Brook Farm

When Annie Smith attends a concert given by popular Christian singer Ryan Jones, all she could do was stare at him. The man standing before her was drop-dead gorgeous, but it wasn't his appearance that had Annie stalled in her tracks. The man before her, that she was so carefully inspecting, closely resembled her husband that she had buried two years earlier. The similarities were not only amazing, they were downright alarming.

Annie soon discovers that Ryan Jones has much more in common with her late husband than just his appearance. When they meet, Annie feels an immediate, unexplainable attraction to Ryan. When the simple touch of their hands in greeting cause an emotional explosion in both of them, Annie feels confused and completely thrown off balance. For a moment, time stood still. The secret was out in the open. A man and woman, on the brink of something that neither anticipated but both understood. There was a connection of their hearts that couldn't be denied.

From Annie's Stony Brook Farm in Boston, to Ryan's ranch in Tennessee, this romantic comedy will sweep you away. Annie is actively pursued by a man full of confidence and godliness. She is still struggling with the pain of losing her husband and the fear of opening her heart up to another. As Annie learns to trust in God in a way that she has never trusted anyone, God heals her heart in a way that only He can do.

Chatfield
Hollow

Chatfield Hollow is the exciting conclusion to Stony Brook Farm. This fast-paced, romantic comedy bounces back and forth between Massachusetts and Tennessee almost as quickly as the teasing and joking do between Annie and Ryan. They both enjoy surprising each other in their own unique and creative ways.

As time goes on, their friendship continues to deepen through their own, honest, heartfelt talks. The time they spend together horseback riding in the mountains, sleigh riding, and attending events together confirms to them that God is healing them from past heartaches and preparing them for the future.

The chemistry between Annie and Ryan intensifies, and they slowly begin to take their relationship in the direction of forever. As a true Cinderella–type wedding is planned, not everyone is happy with their decision, and they are faced with obstacles that could tear them apart.

Through the battles, Annie and Ryan grow closer to the Lord and closer to each other. Annie learns to stand up and face her accusers instead of running away. She comes to realize that Ryan Jones is not only a man worth fighting for, he is a man that she is head-over-heels in love with and doesn't want to live without.

About the Author

Sharon Snow Sirois, a former teacher, has been writing stories all her life. She and her husband have been active in youth ministry for over twenty years. Sharon is an avid reader, who enjoys hiking, sailing, biking and skiing. She is a home schooling mom who lives in Connecticut with her husband and four children.

Sharon loves to hear from her readers. You can write her through Lighthouse Publishing or email her at: sharonsnowsirois @hotmail.com